CAST OF CI

Brenda Davison. With her ash blon
she was the kind of woman men notic
the others she wasn't born with a sp
killed in an airplane accident.

Pete Davison. Her brother-in-law, he has nutmeg red hair, money problems, and likes the west much more than the east. He's seen dancing with Brenda. He's a bit fresh with the ladies but as Jean's friend once remarked "boys who don't whistle after girls at least once in their life don't ever amount to much."

Anne Collier. Pete claims he's going to marry her. She's a stunning goddess of a woman and looks like she ought to be a model in *Vogue*. She's not sure Pete is husband material is very fond of

Katharine Elizabeth (Katy) Davison. Brenda's three-and-half year old daughter. The Davison fortune is mostly in her little hands which may explain why someone tried to kill her and just about everyone wants her to be part of their family.

Elizabeth Ashbrook. A somewhat plain looking woman among these beauties but she has beautiful eyes and is very controlling. She's used to a lavish lifestyle—her first husband stepped out of a window 40 stories up when he ran out of money. She's Brenda's sister-in-law and Pete's sister.

Clive Ashbrook. Elizabeth's second husband. He cuts quite a dashing figure.

Harold (Hal) Crouch. He manages the Davison estate.

Count Felix von Osterholz. .He collapses at Brenda's party but she claims she doesn't know him.

Ellen and Hank Rawlings. Old friends of the Abbotts.

Tony Konrad. Was it only Pat's lavish tips that made this New York cabbie hang around?

Lieutenant-Detective Jeffrey Dorn. An NYPD homicide detective.

Sergeant Goldberg. Another cop, this isn't his first rodeo with the Abbotts.

Paula Eastwood. A Prussian-born beautician who caters to the rich and is said not be adverse to renting her apartment out for romantic encounters.

Dr. Amos Crossland. As Katy's doctor he suspected someone tried to poison the child. He later killed himself but Pat isn't so sure it was suicide.

Dr. Wayland Campbell. He bought Crossland's practice.

Vivian Black. Crossland's nurse.

Pat & Jean Abbotts. He's our detective, she's our narrator.

Books by Frances Crane

Featuring the Abbotts

The Turquoise Shop (1941)
The Golden Box (1942)
The Yellow Violet (1942)
The Pink Umbrella (1943)
The Applegreen Cat (1943)
The Amethyst Spectacles (1944)
The Indigo Necklace (1945)
The Shocking Pink Hat (1946)
The Cinnamon Murder (1946)
Murder on the Purple Water (1947)
Black Cypress (1948)
The Flying Red Horse (1950)
The Daffodil Blonde (1950)
Murder in Blue Street (1951)
The Polkadot Murder (1951)
Murder in Bright Red (1953)
13 White Tulips (1953)
The Coral Princess Murders (1954)
Death in Lilac Time (1955)
Horror on the Ruby X (1956)
The Ultraviolet Widow (1956)
The Buttercup Case (1958)
The Man in Gray (1958)
Death-Wish Green (1960)
The Amber Eyes (1962)
Body Beneath a Mandarin Tree (1965)

*Reprinted by the Rue Morgue Press

Non-Series Mysteries

The Reluctant Sleuth (1961)
Three Days in Hong Kong (1965)
A Very Quiet Murder (1966)
Worse Than a Crime (1968)

Non-Mystery

The Tennessee Poppy, or, Which Way Is Westminster Abbey? (1932)

The Cinnamon Murder

A Pat and Jean Abbott mystery

Frances Crane

Rue Morgue Press
Lyons, Colorado

About Frances Crane

AFTER SHE WAS EXPELLED from Nazi Germany prior to the start of World War II, Frances Kirkwood Crane, recently divorced and with a daughter heading for college, needed to find a new way to make a living. The old market for her writing—primarily poking gentle fun at Brits from the point of view of an American living abroad—was suddenly out of fashion. Americans no longer wanted to laugh at the foibles of the English now that brave little Britain was engaged in a desperate struggle for its very survival against the forces of Hitler.

Up to that point, life had been relatively easy for Frances. Her husband, Ned Crane, was a well-paid advertising executive with the J. Walter Thompson agency, whose dubious claim to immortality was the Old Gold cigarette slogan, "Not a cough in a carload." Frances herself was a regular contributor to a new sophisticated humor magazine called *The New Yorker*. Many of her short sketches for that magazine were collected in book form in 1932 as *The Tennessee Poppy or Which Way Is Westminster Abbey?*

Back in the states, newly divorced and in need of money—living in the United States was more expensive than living in Europe—she had turned to the mystery field at the suggestion of one of her old editors who told her it was a "hot market." Not long after arriving in Taos, New Mexico, Crane, now around 50, heard about an incident involving a jewelry store in that artists' colony, which inspired her first Pat and Jean Abbott mystery, *The Turquoise Shop*, published by Lippincott in 1941. Although she changed the name of town to Santa Maria and even commented that it had not yet been spoiled in the fashion of Taos and Santa Fe, there is absolutely no question that it was based on Taos. In fact, Mona Brandon and her hacienda in *The Turquoise Shop* are loosely based on Mabel Dodge Luhan and her famous adobe home (now a bed and breakfast inn).

Jean Holly (she sounds terribly experienced and world weary, yet she's only 26) meets up with a handsome San Francisco private detective in that first novel. While Jean doesn't do any real sleuthing on her own, she functions as Pat's Watson and her careful observations, some only a woman of that era would make, bear close attention. In the current case, she knows that one of the women has not eloped because "She wouldn't've eloped in a tweed suit she wears mornings on errands. She wouldn't've taken an evening bag with a tweed outfit like that." Observations like that is why the Crane novels made superb use of a female narrator. *The Turquoise Shop* was followed by 25 more books featuring Pat and Jean Abbott, who marry toward the end of the third book, all with a color in the title. The series was so popular that it spun off a radio program, *Abbott Mysteries*, which ran on the Mutual Network in the summers of 1945, 1946 and 1947. Many of them take the Abbotts to locales across the United States and around the world, although they were to return to Santa Maria several times in the course of the series. *The Shocking Pink Hat* takes the Abbotts to San Francisco where is their home base. As usual, the locale is described in loving detail. Crane, who was expelled as a reporter from Germany in the late 1930s because of her open opposition to the Nazi's treatment of Jews, makes her usual quiet observations on race and ethnicity, this time in discussing Chinese-Americans. When Crane has a character describe someone as a "Chink" or use the "N" word in any of her books, you can be sure that he or she isn't going to be sympathetic. Crane's treatment of the Mexicans and Indians in New Mexico is handled in much the same way.

But Crane's intent was not to mount a soapbox. She wrote entertaining detective novels. Crane was quite familiar with the trends in contemporary detective fiction and was extremely well-read in the field. Along with fellow women mystery writers Lenore Glen Offord and Dorothy B. Hughes, she was one of the most influential mystery reviewers in the country, dwarfed in influence only by Anthony Boucher (for whom Bouchercon, the World Mystery Convention, is named). She relished her place in the literary world and numbered among her friends such literary lights as James Jones and Sinclair Lewis as well as her editor at Random House, the very urbane Bennett Cerf. Yet she realized she was not in that same league with these literary heavyweights, remarking once to Cerf that she was but a "minor light."

But all good things seemingly must come to an end. The Abbotts cracked their last case in 1965 with *Body Beneath the Mandarin Tree*. In the 1960s, Crane also wrote five stand-alone mysteries which were published in England but failed to find an American publisher. The last of these, *Worse Than a Crime*, appeared in 1968 when she was 78 years old, and though she would live another 13 years and enjoy relatively good health, her career as a mystery writer was over, and she settled into a well-earned retirement. Yet she had a better run than many women writers of her era, and, unlike most writers, male or female, she earned a good living at it. While many other female mystery writers who began in the 1930s and 1940s saw their careers end with the death of the rental libraries and the advent of the male-oriented paperback original in the early 1950s, Crane not only survived, publishing well into the 1960s, but endured, as any out-of-print book dealer who has ever offered one of her titles in a catalog and been overwhelmed with orders can testify. Her fans don't just enjoy her books, they revel in them, then and now.

She spent much of the last forty years of her life in her adopted New Mexico, mostly in Taos (though the "hippie invasion" in the 1960s drove her eventually to move to Santa Fe). She returned frequently to Lawrenceville to visit family. Three months before her 91st birthday, failing health forced her to enter a nursing home in Albuquerque, where she died on November 6, 1981. She made one final posthumous visit to Lawrenceville, a trip that many old-timers in that town still recall with amusement. The postmaster sent word to her nephew Bob, a local doctor, that a package had arrived for him from New Mexico. "Only," he explained, "you'll have to pick it up yourself. I'm not touching it."

The package was marked "human remains." Bob and other fellow family members scattered the ashes it contained on the family farm. Frances Kirkwood Crane not only came home, she did so in her usual unconventional style.

Note: For additional information on Crane and her connections to Taos read Tom & Enid Schantz' introduction to the Rue Morgue Press edition of *The Turquois Shop*.

The Cinnamon Murder

1

Early in April, just as soon as we could actually believe in our luck, which is to say as soon as the checks from the oil discovered on Patrick's heretofore unexciting, unremunerative, and few, ancestral acres in Wyoming started coming in, we closed up the office in San Francisco temporarily and parked our dachshund, Pancho, and our cat, Toby, with Pat's secretary, and flew East for a vacation.

We stayed at the Waldorf and had a lush time. We spent money like mad. We saw the new shows. We went to the nightclubs. We ate and drank wonderful things in famous places. The fact is we had such a wonderful time that after ten days all we could think of was getting out of there pronto and going some place in the wide open spaces for a real vacation.

We talked it over comfortably on a sofa in Peacock Alley.

"What this family needs is a ranch to live on, Jeanie."

"What this family needs is a family."

"A little girl."

"A boy."

"One of each," Patrick said. "And no more."

"We'll see about that," I said. "Now, that's settled. But it means no more detecting. The detecting business is too dangerous for the father of six children."

"I guess you're right," Patrick said. All at once his attention was wandering.

I jockeyed around in my chair to see what, or rather whom, he was looking at. I said, "While you're in the mood, how about snaring us some plane seats for San Francisco?" No answer. "Hey?" I said.

"A girl just went by who looks as if she belongs in a glade."

So poetic a statement would have been fantastic if he hadn't been right. I looked, and there went a blonde wench I had noticed a few minutes before. She had a small face, a small chin, wide cheekbones and wide-apart hazel eyes. Her hair was the silvery-ash kind. Her braids disappeared under a small artful hat. She wore a dark-green tailleur, dark-green shoes, and she carried a neckpiece of small, expensive-looking furs.

In spite of that water-nymph slant she had chic. The babe in her didn't show at the edges, either, the way it does on a lot of those New York girls. The queerest thing of all was that she walked as if she enjoyed it, not in a desperate panic to get somewhere, which seems typical of even the glamorous females in our metropolis.

The girl disappeared past the picture of Oscar of the Waldorf in the direction of the Alley cafés.

"She's come a long way from the glade," I said. I was jealous.

"Not too long," Patrick said dreamily.

"I seem to have seen her before, Pat."

"Sure. Botticelli painted her, or somebody rather like her. This girl is modern, that's the difference. She's probably got a hunk of Slav in her somewhere to give her those cheekbones. She's dressed by people who know their stuff. She probably smells a lot nicer than a Renaissance Venus, and I'm all for the flatter stomachs you gals have these days. Not to mention your leaner thighs."

"Thanks for including me, dear," I said. I felt hollow inside. I was seething with jealousy. Patrick was usually the few-worded kind. It worried me to hear him gush. "Is there anything she hasn't got, darling?"

Pat's long blue eyes slanted toward me. "Offhand, I'd say you've got more sex appeal in your little finger than she has all over, my amber-eyed sooty-lashed wench!"

I felt pleased but still suspicious. "Well, thanks. How about getting us those plane seats back to San Francisco while we're both in the mood?"

"Here I go, Jeanie. Wait for me here."

He got up. His eyes lingered on the dogwood in the great vases on either side of the portrait of Oscar. He hopes the glade girl will return, I thought. I felt desolate. I watched him stalking along in the opposite direction. He moved slowly, still hoping that she would come back. Or maybe they would meet in the lobby. Maybe she would smile and he would smile back. In his tall, lank, easy-moving way he was certainly the best-looking man in New York, so of course she would want to make his acquaintance. Then what? She was so beautiful.

Forlornly I took out my compact. I checked my make-up. I wondered if I ought to go in for pancake. I eyed critically my yellow eyes and black hair. These New York girls with their super-duper-de-luxe simplicity terrified me. Also, this meant that the artist was stirring again in Patrick. There hadn't been time during the war. It wasn't enough to be tall, lank, blue-eyed and good-looking in the sun-browned sun-lined Western fashion. No! He also had to try to be an artist and even bad artists have models, and wives get old and tiresome while models always stay beautiful and young. Maybe it wasn't such a good idea to retire to a ranch. Sleuthing has its dangers, but what are they compared to the temptations from time on a husband's hands?

"Mrs. Abbott?"

I looked up. It was she. The little furs which made up the neckpiece on her arm were sables. Close up, she had a lovely complexion. Not a hint of pancake.

"Yes?"

She tilted her face. "I'm Brenda Davison. You don't remember me?" I got ready to lie and say I did. "I met you and your husband when you were here a year ago. You were with Ellen Rawlings."

"Oh, yes," I said. She refused to sit down, so I stood up. She was about my height, which is above average. Never in this world had we met this woman anywhere. Seen her, even. I would have remembered her and Patrick would certainly never forget a face like hers.

"I'm in a tearing rush," she said.

"You're the only one in New York who doesn't look it," I said.

"But I am," she said. "I've wasted ten minutes trying to make up my mind to speak to you. I was so afraid you wouldn't remember me. It's lovely that you do. Look—I'm having a party. Just cocktails, nothing important, but I should be so happy if you would come."

"We'd like to," Patrick said.

He had come up behind us. He loathes parties, but he was accepting the invitation without even consulting me.

I smiled amiably.

"Pat, this is Brenda Davison. We met her last year. She knows Ellen Rawlings."

"Oh, of course!" Patrick said. "How are you, Mrs. Davison?"

They shook hands. She hadn't offered hers to me.

I said, "We're sorry we must refuse your invitation, Mrs. Davison. My husband forgets that we're going away."

Brenda Davison looked so let down that I felt horrid. Patrick quickly asked when the party would be. This afternoon, any time after five, Brenda said. Why couldn't we make it? Patrick asked. It was not far, Brenda said then. The address was 531 East 55th, directly on the East River. Sure we could make it, Patrick said. I said, oh, yes, of course. We smiled all the way round and Brenda said good-bye and moved away, walking for all her so-called tearing rush as though she had all the time in the world.

I sat down and took out a cigarette and Patrick gave me a light from his lighter.

"What made you think she was missus, Pat?" I asked, to start with.

"Why wouldn't she be?" Patrick asked back.

"Did you get those tickets?" I asked quickly.

"That I did, Jeanie. We fly tomorrow morning at nine. Think you can make it, dear?"

"I know darn well I can," said I.

Our cab driver was one of those characters who seem to blossom in the taxi business in New York. As he drove us he gave highlights on the sights, on political situations everywhere, on life, on how to be happy though married, on why people ought to have children. He talked about the home he and the wife Bertha were saving up to buy in the Jersey hills. All he needed was three thousand more dollars. Patrick seemed to be doing rather more than his share sometimes to supply that need.

His name was Tony Konrad. He was a plump, bright-eyed crescent-lipped little man. His clothing was a collection of oddities. His devotion to us seemed odd, because his habitual air with others held a cavalier nonchalance. He had four kids, nine grandchildren, and he lived in the Bronx.

My ancestry is heavily Scot. I am skeptic. I thought that Tony's hanging around outside the Waldorf waiting for us to show up might be explained by the money which Patrick, in his San Francisco fashion, lavished as tips. Patrick hasn't a suspicious nature, like me, so he honestly believed that the little man liked us. I kept saying that no one else in New York, that is, no stranger, had taken any interest in us whatever, so it had to be the tips.

At the magnificent white apartment house beside the river Tony bounced out of his seat, opened the door, pocketed Patrick's greenback, and said he would wait around for us.

"Better not," I said. "We may be here a while."

"People coming and going, lady," Tony said. "I pick up some fares."

An oversized doorman in a faun-colored uniform opened the door into the red-carpeted foyer. An elevator as silent and efficient as those at the Waldorf whisked us to a duplex penthouse on the roof. A small, middle-aged man-servant let us in through a massive door which looked like antique oak but was reinforced steel. It closed after us with an impressive zoom, and we were at Mrs. Davison's party.

Despite the splendor which pillowed it, Brenda Davison's party was a rat-race. The people in the hall, the immense living room and the dining room, might have been scooped up from Forty-Second Street and transported here without sorting. What attractive guests there were seemed lost in the herd.

Now, why had she bothered to invite us to this kind of thing? My good-ness! I suggested departing before we got entangled. I was too late. Suddenly, Brenda materialized out of a group which smacked of a corner saloon, and Patrick was gazing at her as though charmed.

She again wore green, a long-skirted dress, and she had a small stiff green bow in the pale thick braids on top of her head. Her hands were white and graceful. She was using a nail-enamel in a very special cinnamon-red. It wouldn't suit everybody, but on Brenda Davison it was chic and remarkable.

"I've been looking for you," she said. We shook hands. I noticed a good many diamonds and sapphires. The sapphire in the ring guarding her wedding ring was the kind you'd pay ten thousand dollars for and not be sorry. "Do you want to meet people, or find your way around?" She didn't wait for an answer. "You'll want a drink. The maids are somewhere with Manhattans or martinis, and you'll find whisky and more cocktails in the dining room. I want you to meet Pete Davison. I don't see him now, but I'll fetch him to you when I do find him." She said then, "Ellen and Hank Rawlings are somewhere, I think."

She sank back into the quagmire of her guests. She was gone.

"Serves you right," I mumbled at Patrick. "Look what you've got us into."

"Want a Manhattan?" he asked, reaching me one from a tray balanced timidly among the bended elbows by an elderly maid. "I think I'll have Scotch. Let's find the dining room."

I spied a French window opening outdoors.

"This place is bringing on my claustrophobia," I said. "You'll find me outside."

Holding my stemmed glass high like a torch I wormed my way out on a terrace.

Here it was lovely. The air was sharp and there was a dampness in it. There were tubs of green boxwood about and the flower-boxes near the balustrade were filled with yellow daffodils.

Dusk was at hand. The sky was tinted. I walked across the terra-cotta tiles to the railing. Straight below spread the East River, dotted with fat tugs and flat barges. The great bridge up to the left soared fantastically over a view otherwise banal, and the whole world seemed to hum and vibrate from its traffic.

The bridge was the heart and the life of this part of New York. It filled me with sudden excitement. I was glad now we had come.

After a few minutes I turned my back on the river to watch for Patrick. I wanted to show him the bridge.

Set back, one story up, was another terrace which must open from the second floor of the penthouse. It was railed, like this one, with a concrete balustrade, and above that was a tall spiked-iron fence.

I was wondering what sort of inmate it accommodated, when a man came out of the drawing room and approached me on this lower terrace. He was tall, young and red-headed, and had dark-gray eyes in a sun-tanned face.

"Hi," he said.

"Hi," I said.

"I'm Pete Davison," he said.

"I'm Jean Abbott."

His eyebrows angled up when he grinned.

"Brenda was right proud of snagging you, Mrs. Abbott. But I'll lay a hundred to your one you didn't know what you were getting into." He jerked a thumb back at the party. "Did you ever see the likes of that?"

"Plenty of times. And so, I guess, have you."

He laughed. "I guess I have. Cigarette?"

I set my cocktail glass on a white metal table and took the cigarette. He gave me a light. "Are you from the West, Mr. Davison?"

"Call me Pete," he said. "They sent me West to school. I somehow never came back, except to my father's funeral four years ago. After that I joined the navy. The navy didn't ask me where I wanted to go, but I wasn't sorry it didn't turn out to be New York. I hope I don't sound unkind to New York, Mrs. Abbott?"

"I guess New York can take it, Mr. Davison."

"The name is Pete."

"All right. But you must call me Jean, then. You have a very beautiful wife, Pete." Up winged the eyebrows. "Don't you remember? Brenda."

His expressive face saddened. "Brenda is my sister-in-law. My brother Jack died around three years ago. He was killed in a plane crash."

"I'm sorry." I was indeed. The memory hurt him.

I liked him. I wished that Patrick would come out so he could meet Pete Davison as well as look at the bridge. I liked his rugged face. I specially liked his red hair. It was thick and in a crew cut, and a beautiful shade, nearer nutmeg than the commoner carrot color. He wore a gray suit, a white shirt, and his necktie was light gray with dark blue. His clothes were good, but he wore them as if he took no interest in them.

"Pat Abbott is famous in the West," he said. "I'm looking forward to meeting him."

"Thank you."

He said, quietly, "Brenda has a little girl, Katy. I'm hoping to talk her into taking Katy home with me." He brandished his cigarette upward at the iron fence. "Katy wouldn't need a corral like that in Arizona."

So Katy was the inmate! "How old is Katy?"

"Three and one half." Pete raised his voice. "Ka-ty?"

A small girl with blue eyes and black pigtails, dressed in a scarlet coat and cap, came and peered down at us through the balusters of the railing below the iron fence.

"Hello, Uncle Pete," she called.

"Hello, Katy. Mrs. Abbott, may I present my niece, Katharine Elizabeth Davison?"

Katy curtsied. "How do you do?" She spoke each word very distinctly.

"How do you do, Katy?"

The child turned to some one out of our view on the upper terrace. "Anne, come quick. Here is Uncle Pete and Mrs. Abbott."

A tall girl in a brown tweed suit and a white sweater came to the upper railing. She had the good shoulders, the straight back, lean flanks, and heavy photogenic hair you see on the models photographed in *Vogue*.

There certainly were beautiful people around this place, in spite of the mixed-up crowd. First the gladelike Brenda. Then Pete. Then the lovely little Katy. And now this stunning goddess of a girl.

"Hi, Annie," Pete said. "Jean Abbott, meet the future Mrs. Pete Davison."

"The name is Anne Collier. How do you do?" said the girl.

Somebody laughed. It was a rough but pleasant laugh and it came from the direction of the living-room door. A tall lean red-headed woman was standing just outside on the terrace. She wore a mink coat, a navy dress, and a hat which was frankly nothing but a lid. Her features were on the rugged side, like Pete's. Her mouth was rather large and her eyes were shaped and colored like green almonds, and they were very beautiful.

Except for the eyes she was plain, but she dominated the good-looking people in this group as completely as the great bridge dominated the view.

She was holding a whisky-and-soda in one hand and in the other was a long black cigarette holder containing half a smoking cigarette.

"There's a brawl or something in the dining room, Pete. I hate to break this up but maybe you'd better come."

It was not a brawl.

A man with thick black eyebrows and auburn hair lay stretched on the deep green carpet in the dining room having a sort of fit. By the time I had worked my way into that room, by finding the route through the kitchen, the guests had been ejected into the hall and the living room and the door between closed.

Patrick was balancing on his heels beside the patient. He was doing the usual things, counting the heartbeat, touching the forehead, lifting the eyelids. He seemed puzzled.

He always looked puzzled at such moments. Poker-faced is a better word.

Even if he knew something special he wouldn't show it.

A slender middle-aged man with gray above his ears and blue eyes and blue veins showing in a high white forehead faced Patrick across the prostrate man, and another tall and very handsome dark man waited discreetly two steps distant. The plain woman with the wonderful eyes fitted a fresh cigarette into the long black holder. Pete Davison fidgeted and looked as if dying to do something. Brenda Davison stood beside Pete Davison with her white hands linked and working. She watched Patrick as if this was a decisive moment in her life.

"Doesn't anyone know him?" Patrick asked. By the way he spoke I knew he had asked it before.

Nobody answered. Then the plain woman laughed.

"This is rather fun, Brenda," she said.

"Fun?" said the blue-eyed man with the gray in his hair. He shook his head at the plain woman. "It won't be fun if he checks out, Liz. Did you get the doctor, Pete?"

"I got him. He said he'd be right up. He said not to move the guy. Not to do anything."

"I don't think he will die," Patrick said. He at no time seemed to lift his eyes from the patient. "At least, not now. He's improving."

"Oh, thank goodness," Brenda said.

She said it with such fervor that the plain woman—Elizabeth—gave her a look full of inquiry, and then she dropped her eyes to her cigarette, which she lighted with a lighter in a gold, gem-encrusted case. She put the lighter into a dowdy suede bag and laid the bag on the dining table. The furniture in the room was Italian Renaissance, either antique or simulated. The period suited Brenda. I wondered if she had planned it herself, or if a decorator had suited the decor to her special kind of beauty.

Easing nearer, I looked at the man on the floor. He would be tallish, with those long legs. His face had a grayish cast. That might be due to the attack, but his cheeks were hollow and his color suggested—what? Hunger? I felt a rush of pity. Drugs? I felt suspicious. His hands were white and so small and thin for his size that they seemed like a woman's.

Patrick unflexed the fingers, first on the right hand and then the left. He was curious about the man, and was checking to see if his hands revealed his occupation. The nails were freshly manicured. The palms were white and soft-looking.

"I wish I knew what ails him," Pete Davison said impatiently.

"It's some sort of heart attack," Patrick answered. He did not look away from the patient.

"Oh, dear!" Brenda cried.

"Who are you?" Elizabeth asked Patrick.

Without looking at her, he said, "My name is Patrick Abbott."

She looked at me. "You're his wife." It was a statement.

I nodded, and the man with the gray in his temples said to Elizabeth, "I was standing by the table yonder talking with Mr. Abbott when this happened, Liz. He's a private detective." The almond-green eyes moved toward the tall handsome dark man and instantly back to the speaker. "I expect it's lucky Mr. Abbott's here. He probably knows as much about a thing like this as most doctors."

"Not that much," Patrick said.

"My God, Clive!" Elizabeth said to the dark man. "A detective? How exciting!"

"Rather," said the tall, dark and handsome man.

"Isn't there really any way to find out who he is?" Elizabeth asked, moving up beside the man with the gray in his hair. "Hal, have Mr. Abbott search him, find out who he is." Without pausing, she said to me, "Mrs. Abbott, have you met Harold Couch? He's our boss. We Davisons never can lift a finger and do any little thing until Hal says so. Hal, what should we do?"

"Exactly what we are doing, Liz. This sort of thing is pretty ticklish."

"Can't we find out who he is? Brenda, are you fibbing? Don't you really know who he is?"

Brenda looked terrified.

"I told you I'd never seen him in all my life, Elizabeth."

"She hasn't the foggiest," Clive Ashbrook said. "We asked her before you and Pete showed up, Liz."

"Well, it's damned unusual, but I hope it ends all right," Elizabeth said. "I'd like to know what his name is. Nosy of me, no doubt, but there you are."

Patrick thrust a hand into the man's inside coat pocket and fetched out a brand-new pigskin wallet. Its entire contents were two one-dollar bills and a small packet of visiting cards. A delicate tissue fluttered down to the green carpet as Patrick extracted one and read, "Count Felix von Osterholz."

Elizabeth Ashbrook lowered her eyelids. She had thick eyelashes, but they were no darker than her skin. They shut out her gorgeous eyes and it was as if she had absented herself from the room, or as if a different woman stood in her place.

She did not speak. She turned away and without lifting the eyes toward us again walked over to a window which looked to the bridge.

Clive Ashbrook's dark, diffident gaze left the man on the floor and fastened itself on his wife.

2

Night had fallen. The lights were winking out in the shadowy towers of the city. There was a small fitful wind. Around Rockefeller Plaza hung the scent of Easter lilies blooming in the formal flower beds. Automobiles moved through the streets almost as though they'd love to linger a little.

This was a pensive and beguiling New York. It fascinated me.

"Darn this town!" I said.

We were strolling up Fifth Avenue, on our way to a late dinner date with Ellen and Hank Rawlings, in their apartment on Central Park South.

Patrick pressed my arm tight against his ribs. It was a habit of his, which I loved, because it made me feel happy and looked after.

"What's the matter with it?" he asked.

"Just when I get fed up to the teeth with the place it turns right around and charms me. It's—why it's colossal!"

"Um-m," Patrick said.

"When we leave New York let's go in the daytime. At night I'd think I was about to miss something."

"We're leaving La Guardia Airport at nine A.M. tomorrow."

"Perfect."

"Um-m."

"I'm afraid you're not listening, darling. You're thinking about something else."

"Another woman," Patrick said.

Brenda Davison's lovely face, her wide-apart hazel eyes and the pale glimmering hair with the gay little green bow nested in its coronet of braids, rose between me and New York.

I said, "I suppose she rouses the artist in you, darling?"

"The parent," Patrick answered. "I'm thinking about Katy Davison." I relaxed. That could be remedied, in due time. "Katy in her high-priced clink."

"The poor little thing," I said. We walked half a block. Then I said, "Pat, that Tony Konrad is tailing us. I'm sure that's his cab which keeps pulling up and stopping across the street every couple of blocks. We can't even take a walk without being chaperoned by a taxi driver."

"He's very handy, scarce as cabs are," Patrick said.

"It may be handy but it doesn't make sense. Nobody but a gangster would take that much interest in anybody in New York."

Patrick laughed and kissed me, right under the streetlight at the corner near De Pinna's, but nobody cared. Nobody bothered to look, even.

"You see? Nobody except the few people we know personally 1 interest in us except Tony. You give him big tips, in your crazy way, but not enough for him to follow us around when we've told him we positively want to walk. Why does he do it? Did you get him sent up or something, some time, Pat?"

"Never," Patrick said. "I think he just likes us, Jeanie."

"Nuts," said I.

We lost Tony when we turned into 58th at Bergdorf's, but after we walked in front of the Plaza Hotel and were on Central Park South, there he was again, crawling along on the other side of the street. As we turned into the Rawlings' apartment house, Patrick flipped a hand in his direction.

I could imagine his plump-lipped, bright-eyed response. Why did he follow us? What did he want?

At the Rawlings', though I was dying to talk about the Davisons, I waited for Patrick to bring up the subject and he let it ride till dinner was over and we were having coffee and drinking calvados, which had been sent to Ellen from France.

"We went to a party this afternoon, Ellen," Patrick said. "At the home of a gal we met through you. Brenda Davison."

Ellen Rawlings is slender, straight-backed, blue-eyed, and has two wings of pure white in her black hair. She sat up a trifle straighter before answering.

"You met Brenda through me? When?"

"Last year," Patrick said.

"I didn't know Brenda last year," Ellen said. "I've known her sister-in-law, Elizabeth Ashbrook, for ages, used to see her and Clive in Paris before the war. I met Brenda about three months ago when a young friend of ours, Anne Collier, went to stay with Brenda's child."

"Is Anne still there?" Hank asked Ellen.

Ellen frowned. "I'm afraid she's in rather a spot. She's got attached to Katy and she seems to feel that something awful will happen to her if she leaves."

"What could happen?" I asked.

Ellen said, "I don't know exactly. Anne doesn't say."

"Katy has too much money," Hank said.

"Perhaps they all have," I said.

Hank said, "It's an estate. The Davison who made the money—Elizabeth's father—tied it up so his own children couldn't throw it around. Seems he'd rather take a chance on his prospective grandchildren, if there were any. The money is all managed and paid out according to the will by Harold Couch."

"We met him at the party."

"He's it. Nice guy. I'd hate to have his job, if the other estates he handles are as much trouble as the Davison estate."

"He seemed nice," I said.

"He's okay," Hank said.

Ellen said, "Old Mr. Davison sowed trouble for his children. There ought to be some way to break that will. It's unfair to Elizabeth and the younger brother, Pete. Did you meet Pete? He's most attractive."

"Does Katy have more than the others?" I asked.

"Much more, apparently. And she wasn't even born when her grandfather fixed up the will. Liz claims that her father made the will after he knew she never could have children, so she contends that it was a deliberate act to deprive her of a fair share of the estate."

"She doesn't complain," Hank said. "She's rather funny about it, as a matter of fact."

"We met her at the party," I said. "She's—well, she's a woman you'd never forget."

"Rather," Ellen said. "I feel sorry for that little Katy, I really do. She was ill in the winter and they all got in a perfect tizzy over it. Brenda let her nurse go, and even the servants. The nurse had been with Katy since she was born, but for some reason she had to go. It was all very hush-hush. That's when Anne went to stay with Katy till the nurse was replaced. They haven't found anyone. I think Brenda is rather overwhelmed by Liz and wants to please her, and that Liz wants to keep out of it to avoid complications. I don't know. That's just an idea."

"What was wrong with Katy?"

"I've no idea. Nothing alarming, perhaps. If Katy weren't so rich there might not have been any fuss. Their doctor died just then, too, which didn't help."

"They're the kind of people who have to be taken care of," Hank said. "The right agent. The right doctor. All that sort of thing. Bores me, if you really want to know."

"What was wrong with the doctor?" Patrick asked.

Ellen said, "He shot himself."

Hank was looking at me. He spied my suspiciousness and grinned and said, "Nothing fishy about it, Jean. The doctor shot himself in his own office with his own gun. It just happened to coincide with Katy's illness."

Ellen said, "Just at that time Anne Collier was staying with us while looking for a job. She's a friend of Susan's." Susan was Ellen's daughter, now twenty-two. "Elizabeth Ashbrook phoned me—I think she called everybody she knew—asking if I knew of someone trustworthy who would stay with the child temporarily, and I suggested Anne. I'm sorry I let Anne in for it.

The whole situation worries her too much."

"In what way?"

"She's frightened for the child. And for Brenda, too. I think it's rather ridiculous. Frankly, I think Brenda works on Anne's sympathy. Anne has made up her mind that Elizabeth is rather sinister, I'm afraid."

"I'd hate to have Elizabeth for my in-law," I said. "She's rather terrific, if you know what I mean."

Hank said, "Elizabeth's okay. The way she lives takes more money than she gets from the estate, apparently. Maybe she gets panicked. Another drink?" He went round with the apple brandy. "Elizabeth married two men her father didn't approve of. That's why he drew up that will."

"Her present husband is most attractive," I said. "He was at the party."

"Very, very handsome," said Ellen.

"Clive's okay," Hank said. "He hasn't any profession or any sort of job and old Mr. Davison was a self-made magnate and he didn't approve of that sort of guy. He didn't approve of Jim Emmerman, her first, either."

"Elizabeth wouldn't want a husband who worked," Ellen said. "She wants Clive around all the time. I think they have a good time."

"Depends on what you call work," Hank said. "She keeps Clive busy as hell just running after her. He likes it, apparently. But to do nothing year in and year out without being bored takes money for people like the Ashbrooks. And if she had a fair portion of the income from the estate they could do everything they like."

"They could anyway, if they weren't so extravagant," Ellen said. "They insist on living beyond their means."

"She doesn't look extravagant," I said.

"Well," Ellen said, "she is. I like her, you know. But, as you said a while ago, she's rather terrific. Too much personality or something. Most people are a little in awe of Liz Ashbrook."

I saw her as that first time, when she stood on the terrace, laughing, her highball glass in one hand, her cigarette holder in the other, her green eyes taking everything in. I remembered the hushed moment.

"Tell the Abbotts about Liz's first marriage," Hank said.

Ellen considered it, since she doesn't much like gossip, then said, "Her first husband was Jim Emmerman, who was very rich. Oil, I think. They had a grand wedding and old Mr. Davison's present to Elizabeth was a wonderful string of matched pearls. They were reputed to have come from the Hapsburg crown jewels and were valued at something like half a million dollars. Liz and Jim had a gay time. They lived as she and Clive do, in the best hotels, and most of the time they were in Europe. Jim drank like a fish. Then Elizabeth started having tremendous affairs. She would tell you about them herself, so I don't feel I'm saying anything I shouldn't."

"Oh, we'll probably never see her again," I said.

"Elizabeth was very dressy then. You've seen her? She never was really pretty. But, in a way, she had beauty. In London and Paris they liked her looks. People thought she was a personality. She was dressed in rather bizarre clothes by a great dressmaker and she was known as a wit. Anyway, finally, she met Clive Ashbrook. They fell in love."

"Jim meanwhile had used up his dough," Hank said. "He didn't stay in the States enough to look after his affairs, I guess. Or maybe they spent all of it. Anyhow, they came back to New York for a longer stay than usual, and one afternoon Jim opened a window of the hotel suite they were occupying at that time and waved a hand at Elizabeth and stepped out. It was forty stories up."

Ellen said, "It really happened just like that. Liz was having two or three people in for drinks and they all saw it happen. They all got hysterical and sick, except Liz. After a minute she got up and went to the phone and calmly called the desk and told a clerk what had happened and asked him to do what was necessary."

"She went back to Paris," Hank said. "A year or two before the war started she married Clive Ashbrook."

I asked, "What happened to the pearls?"

"Oh, Elizabeth had sold them years before that. She needed the money."

"Is she much older than Pete?"

"Fourteen or fifteen years, I think. Jack and Peter came fairly close together, but Elizabeth was already nine or ten or more when Jack was born. Their mother died when Pete was still a baby."

Patrick said, "There was an incident at the party. A man named Felix von Osterholz had a heart attack." Again I saw glances meet, and spring apart, but neither Hank nor Ellen commented. "Pete called a doctor who has his office on the ground floor of the apartment house. By the time he arrived the man was able to be moved, and we took him down in the service elevator. Pete and I, Mr. Couch and the doctor. I stopped to ask about him when Jean and I left the party. The doctor said that immediately after we left his office the man asked for a cab and left. There's nothing much to all that, of course, except that nobody seemed to know who he was—none of the family, I mean."

Ellen looked thoughtful, then said, "Anne said that Brenda had been very annoyed lately with gate-crashers. She doesn't know how to cope with such people, apparently."

"Evidently this was one," I said.

"How did you know his name?" Ellen asked.

"He had some engraved cards in his billfold. Very new cards."

There was a tiny interval, then Ellen said, "Don't you think Brenda is beautiful?"

"She's exquisite," Patrick said.

I looked at him. Exquisite is not one of his words.

Hank said, "She sure is!"

I said flatly, "Look, just what is wrong with Brenda Davison? Anybody that beautiful ought not to worry about anything in this world."

Neither replied for a moment, and then Ellen said, "I think Brenda is rather bewildered. Frankly, Elizabeth is pretty strong medicine for a girl like that. Not that she would do anything deliberately, but—well, you know how it is."

"She was a working girl before she married Jack," Hank said. "Even Jack was strong stuff for a girl like Brenda, but he was crazy about her. Elizabeth probably isn't."

3

As we came out of the elevator after leaving the Rawlings' a man just entering the foyer snapped down his hat-brim and went right out again.

The door was the revolving kind. He stayed in his section till he was back on the sidewalk. He was tall and wore a light-colored belted trench-style coat. There was no time to notice more. Besides it was then unimportant.

By the time we were outside he had vanished. There was no tall man wearing a light coat in sight.

Flat-faced dark-windowed buildings flanked the sidewalk. Each had its entrance. Some had shops with set-back entrances to lengthen display windows. He could have ducked into one of these. Or he might have been just a man who had accidentally started into the wrong apartment house and gone out and on into the next by the time we emerged.

The atmosphere was again changed. The wind had ceased. A haze clung to the tops of the buildings. It was thickish. A few hundred feet up and at street level it did not affect visibility other than to give ordinary things glamour. A slight and agreeable dampness softened the air. The pavements glistened.

I slipped my arm through Pat's.

"New York is like a big cat. It's feline. It never really sleeps. It relaxes and dozes, but you feel that it may spring alive any minute. It kind of terrifies you." He didn't say anything. "You read in novels about empty streets making Paris or London seem like cities of the dead. You could never say that of New York."

"I like the place, Jean."

"I adore it at night. But I wish just when you think you're hep to its quaint native customs it wouldn't turn right around and be different."

We had come as far as the Plaza. We always found it hard to pass the Plaza at any time of day without going in, if only for a moment. We entered. A couple of minutes later we were saying how lucky we were to pick up such a good table in the Persian Room without reserving ahead.

Patrick gave our order and I slipped off the fur jacket our oil-money had paid for and glanced at the dancing.

Immediately I saw Brenda Davison. She wore a chiffon evening dress in a stunning Schiaparelli blue. Her hands and wrists were crowded with sapphires and diamonds. She danced with her small flat-cheeked face pressed against the midnight-blue sleeve of her partner's dinner coat. Her eyes were closed. She looked blissfully happy.

Her partner was Peter Davison!

He was not the blithe-talking gay-looking Pete who had seemed to adore little Katy and loved teasing Anne Collier. He seemed serious, grim even. He danced well, but his mind was obviously not on his dancing. Brenda looked transported. Pete looked determined.

All at once, he too became baffling and mysterious. Was he also a violent and extravagant creature like his sister Liz? Why had he come to New York? Was Brenda in love with him?

The orchestra took a breather. The dancers melted away to their tables. Neither of us saw Pete and Brenda again.

It was a quarter of two when we left the Plaza by way of the wide short flight leading into Central Park South. The haze was still just heavy enough to give the scene mystery and charm. The usual row of horse carriages was drawn up at the usual curb. The horses stood with their heads drooping. The drivers sat in dark huddles on their boxes, looking for all the world like bundles of old clothes. Across the street Central Park was silent and alluring.

It was I who proposed a carriage ride. Patrick agreed, to please me, and we started across the street toward the carriages.

A taxi slid up. The driver was Tony Konrad.

"Want to go home now, sir?" He added, "And lady?"

I pressed Patrick's arm, meaning No. And as always whenever Tony showed up I felt suspicious.

"Not now, Tony. I'm about to take my girl for a drive in the park."

"Not a nice night, Bud," Tony said. Sometimes Patrick was Bud, or Brother, or even Pat. I was always Lady.

"You're right, Tony. But we're going just the same."

We waved and walked away. "I don't trust him," I said.

"He's all right," Patrick said.

"He shows up all over. It doesn't make sense. Sometimes you're wrong about people, Pat."

The cab we took was probably the most smelly in the rank, and our driver was an ageless mound of wrappings who didn't seem to care whether we took his cab or not. He steered his nag into the Park and then let it take its own course.

We were immediately glad that we'd come. The Park in this light was enchanting. There was a pleasant absence of traffic, thanks as much to the haze as to the late hour. We lit cigarettes. I settled back in the circle of Patrick's long arm. The horse ambled along. If it hadn't looked so fat and pampered I would have felt sorry for it. Like its driver, it was superbly indifferent to anything around us.

Once in a while a car with its dimmers on would come up behind, scoop us briefly into a basket of soft light, and then pass us. Afterwards the darkness would be deep and exciting. There was one-way traffic, so we met no one. The silence was precious.

"This was a good idea, after all, Jeanie."

"It's been a lovely evening."

"Do you want to stay on a few days? We can change our reservations."

"Nope. I want to leave New York at nine o'clock tomorrow morning, after this lovely night."

For several minutes no one overtook us. The queer thin haze wrapped the rocks and shrubbery in silvery mystery.

Then a car came up which did not pass. It dimmed to its parking lights after picking us up, and fell in about half a block behind, keeping as we did, to the very edge of the driveway. It was irritating.

"I suppose that's your friend Tony."

"If it is," Pat said, "he's overdoing it. There's a time for everything."

"Don't tell me you're disillusioned?"

"I shouldn't wonder," Patrick said. He twisted his head for a look through the little window in the upholstered back of the carriage.

"Let's stop this thing and let him go on ahead."

"Maybe it's not Tony. There's an exit from the Park just ahead somewhere, not far along now. Maybe they're slowing down for that."

"Just how far?"

"It's above the Metropolitan Museum. I don't know exactly how far it is from here because I don't know exactly where we are. You're not worried, are you, dear?"

Of course not, I lied. I was worried and so maybe was he. He didn't want to stop the carriage because he knew that a slow pace was better than none.

He pulled my head back on his shoulder and kissed me. "You're my girl," he said.

We jogged around a curve.

The car did not follow us around the curve. It had apparently stopped and parked. "You see, just a guy like me with his girl!" Patrick said.

We arrived then at a small hill. It was nothing but a longish incline, too slight to be called a hill, but the indolent creature which pulled the carriage took the opportunity to slow down to a lazy walk. The driver paid no heed. He sat in his huddle of old clothes and left what thinking there was to the horse.

Two minutes later the car closed in, using full headlights. Suddenly Patrick talked fast in a low authoritative tone. If it was a stick-up I was to hand over my stuff. Yes, all of it. It was insured. Nope, I wasn't to slip my engagement emerald into the toe of my nylon. Emeralds could be replaced.

Then the car fell back as abruptly as it had come up on us, dimming its lights, and through the little rear window we saw that a second car had come up and was following the first. Almost at once an arrow ahead pointed to the exit above the Museum.

Then the first car sped up and passed us and left the Park. The second, a taxicab, followed the first.

In the comfortable quiet we sat and laughed. The horse clopped on. All that was left to remind us of our alarm was a rather stronger than usual odor of gasoline. We felt not only amused but refreshed. We laughed a lot.

"I imagined things, Pat."

"*You* imagined things? How about me? But maybe we'd better leave the Park ourselves and drive back along Fifth Avenue. My imagination wouldn't act up if it weren't such a good night for a stick-up."

"Nope," I said. "The best part's ahead. Besides, it might unhinge our driver if we change our route."

"You mean the horse."

We laughed as the carriage rolled past the exit, and then the entrance from Fifth Avenue just above it. We felt very merry. We kept laughing because now to be afraid was absurd. We arrived at another miniature hill. The horse slowed to take it easy. A pyramid of rocks rose on the right. On the left the shrubbery was taller than usual, and dense. The only light in sight was a street lamp some distance on, at the top of the slope.

We laughed as the lazy horse managed to take it specially slowly. The beast crawled.

We were halfway up the slope when the big black sedan swooped up behind us and cut in just ahead, with a sharp jamming of brakes. The horse reared and screamed and swerved toward the rocks.

Before the lights of the car were dimmed we saw in silhouette a tall man get out of the seat beside the driver and crouch in the car's shadow as he moved toward us. He wore a light-colored coat.

Our driver leaped off the box and seized the bridle of the horse. The animal kept whimpering and shivering.

Patrick pushed me into my corner of the carriage. His body made a barrier between me and what was now the only exit. On my side the carriage was forced against the rocks.

The crouching figure in the light belted coat straightened up just outside the carriage. He had a gun. He held the gun leveled on us.

The motor of the car kept purring along. Our driver ignored everything except the horse. He stood whispering to and stroking the frightened horse. He kept his back turned as though he didn't know or didn't care what happened to us. My heart kept pounding so hard that you'd've thought the man could hear it.

Suddenly I realized how much to our advantage was our silence. The man couldn't take definite aim because he couldn't make out exactly where we sat in the deep darkness within the carriage.

Uncertain suddenly, anxious not to do the wrong thing, the man moved a step closer. His fatal error! He placed himself within Patrick's long reach and Patrick tried a desperate expedient. His right hand shot forward and gripped the cylinder of the revolver. It could not turn. Therefore the man could not shoot.

I watched the queer deadly silent struggle that ensued with horror. I loathe guns. It was like hands wrestling with a snake. A battle of hands and wrists, of slit eyes and quick breathing.

It ended abruptly. A car was coming. With a tremendous yank the man got possession of his gun and shot back to the waiting car. By the time the second car slid up beside us the sedan's ruby tail lights were vanishing suavely over the hill.

"Something happen, Bud?" Tony Konrad asked from his cab.

"Hello, Tony," Patrick said. He had got out of the carriage.

"Maybe I better drive you back now to the Waldorf?"

"Maybe you had."

Now I was really frightened. As Patrick helped me out I declared that I wouldn't ride in that cab. Why was Tony here? How come he turned up everywhere we went?

"I tailed you, Lady," Tony said.

"Why?"

"I like you, Bud and Lady."

"Well, that's fine," Patrick said. "We like you, too. Just a minute till I square things with this driver."

I was speechless, with terror plus rage, when Patrick put me in the cab. "You're crazy!" I whispered, as Tony drove on in the direction taken by the sedan. Soon he took a left turn and we rolled down Fifth Avenue toward Fifty-Ninth Street. As he drove he explained. He had, he said, seen a tall guy with red hair tail us when we left the Waldorf and walked to Central Park South. So he tailed the guy. He said he had always wanted to be a dick, but there wasn't enough dough in it for Bertha and the kids. The tall guy went into a cigar store and made a phone call after we went into the Rawlings' apartment. Pretty soon a little guy drove up in a black sedan. The tall guy got in. They parked half a block away and waited. The tall guy was restless. He got out of the car every now and then and prowled around. When we went into the Plaza the sedan drove away. Tony didn't see it again till it followed us into the Park.

"And where were you all evening?" I asked.

"I parked my cab on Fifty-Eighth, and hung around. When you came out of the Plaza the guys wasn't around any more so far as I could see and I was about to call it a day when I saw them roll up and turn into the Park. You could be two dead ducks in that old crate of a horse-cab, see, so I buzzed along after the sedan. I almost lost them though when they left the Park, there at the Museum. A red light caught me, but I guessed what they was up to, so when I could I turned around and drove back to the Park."

He is lying, I thought. It doesn't make sense.

"And why do you think we were being tailed?" I asked coldly.

"Maybe you wear too much ice, Lady," Tony said.

That tied it! My ice was limited to a few emeralds which were very dear to my heart, but were nothing to make a couple of gunmen hang around after us all evening. Specially in New York. If they wanted ice they had much better concentrate on somebody like Brenda Davison.

When we got out at the Waldorf Patrick gave Tony a bill. "Buy Bertha a present," he said. Tony thanked him profusely. I felt furious. I thought he had somehow played us for suckers and I said so as we walked under the awning and up the steps. That hundred you just gave him, I said, as we crossed the foyer to the accompaniment of Viennese waltzes from the Wedgwood Room, wasn't enough if he saved our lives, and much too much if he framed us with a phony stick-up. Patrick agreed. He was agreeing with me because he hates to argue and that annoyed me more.

We walked between tall pillars into Peacock Alley. Brenda Davison was sitting on the sofa where we had sat when we saw her for the first time this afternoon. She had a coat of silver-blue mink over her violet-blue evening dress. She rose swiftly when she saw us.

"I've been waiting for you," she said.

4

We sat with Brenda at a table with a banquette along one end and one side, in one of the cafés off Peacock Alley. Patrick sat at the end of the table and I beside Brenda. The shining cinnamon-red of her nail polish set off her white hands and also her jewels. I expect cinnamon-red sounds unattractive. It was, on the contrary, charming. There would be a little black in the blend perhaps. It was a shade for silvery blondes, either with or without that hint of the glade. It is usual for an ash-blonde to fall into the habit of accepted colors in the way of clothes and make-up. Brenda's departure from the pattern was refreshing.

Save for the bar-men and a couple of waiters, and a man and a woman in a far corner, the café was empty, probably because of the time, which was after two in the morning.

Brenda's wide-spaced eyes were watchful. There was a humble quality in her now which did not belong with such beauty.

"I lied to you yesterday afternoon," she said. She had asked for coffee. Patrick usually drinks Scotch, and I had settled, in deference to the hour, for orange juice. "I never met you before. And I did not ask the Rawlings to my party. They don't care for that sort of thing. I lied when I told you they were somewhere around."

"That doesn't seem very serious," Patrick said.

Brenda said, "But I'm scared." She lifted her face to him and said, "At this minute I should like a drink. I wouldn't dare! Somebody might see me having it, and the story would get about and perhaps I would lose my child."

"Why not have a Scotch or brandy in a coffee cup?"

"No, no, I don't dare. It would be noticed. It always is. I am endlessly followed and spied on."

"Suppose someone sees you here? With us? I'm a detective, you know."

"I shall say you are my friends, and that we were having a nightcap. Coffee was my choice. In a pinch I can prove it by the waiter."

I glanced at Patrick. He avoided my eyes. He didn't want Brenda to see us exchanging glances.

"How did you know who we were?" he asked, meaning last afternoon, when she had spoken to us.

"I asked for you at the desk. The clerk happened to know you and said he thought you were somewhere in the lobby. I gave a bellboy some money and he pointed you out. Then I walked by several times trying to get up the nerve to speak to you. When I did—well, I couldn't bring myself to tell you what I wanted right off. So I asked you to my party, thinking that there would be a chance there, somehow, to have a heart-to-heart talk."

I gave my head a tiny shake, specially for Patrick. He saw it, he sees everything, but he gave me no sign.

Look out for this glamorous blonde, I wanted to say. Be careful.

"Anne Collier, who lives with us now, heard about you from Ellen Rawlings," Brenda said. "She asked Ellen where you were stopping, and that's how I happened to come." The cinnamon nails gleamed as her hand fidgeted with her cup. She had not touched the coffee. "I come from a wonderful family," she said. "Of course my father lost everything in the depression, but what difference does that make? Why should having been poor make people in New York think you are common, Mr. Abbott?"

She launched forth in a panegyric about her splendid family. For heaven's sake, I thought, as Patrick, with never a glance at me, sat gravely listening. As she talked about her family her entire manner changed. Her voice became pretentious and rather shrill.

"Where is your family?" I asked.

Aware of me briefly, she said, with an artificial sigh, "They're all dead. I'm the only one left." She turned back to Patrick. "After all, who are the Davisons? Mr. Davison made a lot of money and therefore they could live splendidly in New York and Elizabeth could have a debut. She married a rich man and lived a lot in Europe. She's had advantages. Not because her family's good, which it most certainly is not. But because she's had money, and knew what she wanted to get with it. Clive is different. Clive Ashbrook comes from one of the best old families in New York. His people are real society, and yet he's simple as an old shoe. But Liz—Elizabeth—why does she think she can queen it over me?"

I wished I could catch Patrick's eye. We were wasting our time. He knew it, of course, but no doubt he thought he could put up with her conversation just to look at her.

"Don't you like Elizabeth?" I asked. I was interested in Elizabeth.

The hazel eyes turned to me, and hurried back to my husband. She said, "Oh, yes. Of course I do! Why not?" She asked then, "Do you think violent deaths run in families, Mr. Abbott?"

"No," he said gravely. Just as if her question amounted to something and required a careful answer.

"I'm so glad! I've been so terribly worried for Katy on that account. Her father died in an airplane accident. Did you know that? When Katy was so ill, and when Dr. Crossland died . . . He was our doctor. He shot himself. Another violent death."

"He wasn't a member of your family?"

"No. Oh, no." Brenda stopped talking and gazed absently into her cup.

"Violent deaths sometimes gang up," Patrick said. "Naturally, people then get the idea it's fate. I believe the insurance people have an explanation. The bereaved are distracted and depressed and in spells of absent-mindedness do things like falling downstairs or stepping in front of moving cars."

Brenda was not listening. He was wasting his breath.

"Elizabeth wants my child," she said.

Then she looked simply terrified, as though having made a plain easy-to-understand statement was a serious thing. She glanced all around. The waiter stood at a distance, looking out into Peacock Alley. The only bar-man visible was polishing a cocktail glass. The couple who had been the only other customers had gone.

"I shouldn't've said that. I don't really know," Brenda said.

"Your sister-in-law probably loves Katy. I understand she has none of her own."

"Oh, I don't think it's the money entirely. I'll say that. She's maternal, though you wouldn't think it. She almost died two or three times trying to have a baby—or so they say. Of course, you never know for sure. Nobody really understands Elizabeth. And she always gets what she wants."

Patrick's smile encouraged her.

"She was the one who got me to come here in the first place. I did not want to come to New York. I was talked into coming. Elizabeth said I ought to be here, since Katy is the only child in the family. Our agent, Mr. Couch, agreed with her. Pete was away, in the navy." She frowned. "Now Pete wants me to take her away. He wants her in Arizona. He—he wants to marry me. Oh, you must not tell that, will you not? I am all upset and worried all the time. When Katy was ill I was frantic. I dismissed her nurse. I sent away all the servants. Dr. Crossland was so queer. He was suspicious." She went off into a little silence. A glass clinked on the bar. One of the uniformed guards forever patrolling the Waldorf strolled through the café. He had crossed the room and gone out before Brenda murmured, "Of course, there is the money. That is really what is back of it all."

Patrick said, "What is it you think I can do to help you?"

"Oh, I don't know," Brenda cried, and her hands worked with her coffee cup.

"Let's get you some cognac," Patrick said.

"Oh, no!" she said, and she lifted the cup and drank some of the coffee.

Bewildered, Ellen Rawlings had said. Nuts would have been more like it. I hadn't even proper sympathy. I was merely annoyed.

"If I were—out of the way," Brenda murmured, "Liz would have Katy. Liz would know what to do. She could give her social advantages. Pete says that's crazy. He says by the time Katy grows up what Liz calls social will belong to the dead past. If Katy were out west on a ranch she could have a happy childhood, Pete says. He calls my apartment a glorified birdcage." She smiled for the first time, then said, "Pete is sweet. He's so like Jack, my husband. But Liz will never stand for my taking my baby west. Liz will have me murdered before she will stand for my taking Katy away."

Oh, fiddlesticks, I thought. Nuts!

"Where did you live before coming to New York?" Patrick asked.

"In Chicago. I brought Katy here after Jack died—because of the social advantages. I did it to please Liz. Of course if—if anything should happen to me . . ." she paused. "Have you heard about the money? How so much of it comes to Katy that the others haven't enough? You don't think I can help that, do you? It's in the will. Everything is in that will. I didn't write the will. I don't see why anyone should blame me. Do you?"

Patrick said, making a sudden disgression, "Is it true you had never before seen that man who had a heart attack at your place? Felix von Osterholz?"

Brenda waited to answer.

"I haven't a good memory for people," she said. "I do hope you don't think I invited all those people to that party. I did not. Many of them just came. That sort of thing keeps happening."

"That was why you asked us to come, wasn't it? You wanted me to be there if the uninvited people came?"

"That's why. That was one reason I asked you."

"How long has that sort of thing been going on?"

"I don't know. Quite a while, I think."

"How many of those people were invited?"

"Oh, not many. Not more than half, I think. I asked them because of Pete. I don't give parties often. I invited Pete's friends and Elizabeth's. I don't have any myself. That is—well, I'm rather a friendly person, I like lots of people, but I do want to please Liz, so I never ask my own friends to a party. I hadn't had any party for several months. I stopped having them because . . ."

She paused again and Patrick asked, "Because of gatecrashers?"

"Yes. It always happens. I don't know why. Of course, it is like being careful about a drink, or anything, because if I do anything I shouldn't—or people think I shouldn't—I shall lose Katy. That's why I worry about gate-crashers."

"Oh, for goodness' sakes!" I said. Brenda looked at me as though she'd forgotten I existed. "You sound absolutely—Victorian. After all . . ."

I stopped. Patrick was frowning at me.

"Liz is very old-fashioned about children," Brenda explained. "She's very firm. You'd never think it to see her and hear her talk. She's pretty rugged, you know. But a child! That's different. Katy must be in bed by six, must do this and that, must learn certain manners that would seem kind of queer to my family. As I said, my family is wonderful, but they're unconventional. They think a child should be company. They like to have them around. Liz thinks Katy ought to live all by herself—oh, with her nurse, of course—and me seeing her at lunch and looking in only for a short time in the afternoon. . . . I don't know."

My family *is*, I was thinking. *Bewildered* might be the word.

Brenda said, "I think somebody is trying to kill me."

It was the driest and most direct statement she had made. It was absurd, from her. Neither of us spoke.

"I think the poison Katy got was meant for me."

"So Katy was poisoned?" Patrick said. "You mean when she was ill?"

"Oh, Mr. Abbott! Now I've said it. I have said it right out. Not that it was poison exactly."

"Don't worry about that," Patrick said. "Did anyone think so besides you?"

"Yes, Dr. Crossland."

"The one who shot himself?"

"Yes. He knew. I know he did. He told me to get rid of the nurse. Isn't it funny? We haven't seen her since. She seems to have vanished, really. The servants—he said, let them go. You must do everything for her yourself, he said. I said Elizabeth wouldn't like that. He said the hell with Elizabeth. There's a kitchenette on the second floor of our apartment. It's used only for Katy. She always lunched with me downstairs but the nurse fixed her breakfast and supper upstairs. Now we lunch up with her because I must fix everything she eats myself. The servants never cook for Katy. I won't even let Anne touch anything intended for Katy. Not that I'm afraid of Anne, but I don't want Anne accused."

"You had had Dr. Crossland long?"

"Oh, always since being in New York. He's the family doctor, and Liz said we must have him. We were glad, of course. You see—there's an allergy of some kind—only it's not really an allergy . . ." One of her rings was a circle of diamonds holding a minute watch. She glanced at it. "I must go."

Patrick beckoned the waiter.

"We'll see you home, Mrs. Davison."

"Oh, no. But thank you. Pete is waiting for me with a cab. He's probably furious that I've taken such a time, but he'll wait because he wanted me to see you."

"Pete wanted you to talk to us?"

Her face changed. "You won't mention that, will you? Thank you. I'll phone you in the morning, if I may."

"Yes. Do."

She hurried out. Patrick sat down again after seeing her to the exit from the café, and when the waiter came ordered another Scotch. I had a brandy.

"I need this, after that. Beautiful but bats."

"Could be, maybe."

"That wonderful family! All dead at the beginning of the chapter and later on not all dead. Or something."

"Um-m."

"Do you really think Pete wants to marry her? There was something—when he looked at Anne yesterday afternoon."

"You're our love expert," Patrick said.

"You're hedging, darling."

"She's very beautiful, my dear!"

"She ought to be stuffed and put somewhere on view where she couldn't talk. It's a shame to spoil the illusion."

Patrick said, "All that's really wrong is that she's scared."

"All that's wrong is that she ought to go back where she came from, Patrick."

"I think you've got something there."

"I know I've got something. Brenda is just a plain gal probably from the wrong side of the tracks—but not very wrong side—who has bitten off more than she can chew."

"That's often pretty serious," Patrick said.

"Would you think so if she weren't so *exquisite*?"

"I might think so," Patrick said. "But I wouldn't be so anxious to do something about it."

"You're not going to, I hope?"

"Maybe." The waiter set down the drinks and added them to the check. When he was gone, Patrick said, "Why is she mixed up like that? Why is so scared? Well, I'm scared myself. Look at what's happened. We accept her invitation to her apartment. A man has a phony heart attack. . . ."

"Whoever heard of a phony heart attack?"

"Plenty of draft-dodgers tried it. But why did von Osterholz do it? If that is what it was? And why all the gatecrashers? Why was Katy ill? Why did Dr. Crossland shoot himself? It's a rare doctor who commits suicide. And when they do, it's almost always because they have some fatal illness or other."

"Maybe he had."

"Maybe. But what about the Patrick Abbotts? Why, after going to her party, are we tailed all evening and finally ambushed in Central Park?"

I laughed. It was clear as a bell, that part.

"Darling, Tony Konrad fixed that up, and I know it. I've warned you not to carry so much cash around all the time. This isn't San Francisco."

Patrick said quietly, "The man with the gun in the Park was von Osterholz."

I didn't say anything for a moment.

"Are you sure?"

"Practically sure."

"Did you see his eyebrows?"

"Nope. It was too dark. His hat was pulled down."

"Then how do you know?"

"I—know."

"That settles it, Pat. We catch the nine o'clock plane!"

Patrick did not answer. He paid the bill. We crossed Peacock Alley into the main lobby. He went to the desk to get our key. I strolled along past the place where you buy theatre tickets meaning to meet him near the elevators.

I happened to notice the time: 2:25.

Then I saw Pete Davison.

He was standing just outside the lobby, near the telephone booths. He was watching Patrick at the desk getting our key.

As Patrick turned, so that he might have seen Pete, the latter went quickly into a telephone booth. I mentioned this to Patrick after we stepped into the elevator cage.

"He took Brenda home and got back in a hurry," I said.

"He had at least ten minutes."

"That's not enough."

"It could be."

We made a swift ascent to our lofty floor. We walked soundlessly on the deep carpet along the hall. We exchanged nods with another one of the uniformed men who patrol the hotel. We turned into our corridor.

Our room was at the end. It had an outside door, a small vestibule or entrance hall, and an inner door. Patrick unlocked the outer door.

The telephone in the room started ringing.

A slip of paper lay on the floor of the vestibule. I stooped and picked it up and followed Patrick into the bedroom. I had left both doors open. The room was dimly lit from the lighted corridor. As I reached for the light switch I saw Patrick rounding the foot of the bed to answer the phone.

My hand didn't make contact with the switch. Suddenly I was pushed forward violently and I fell headlong. A shape leaped over me. I heard a thud. After a moment the doors closed. One, then the second. There was darkness and silence.

5

My face crowded the carpet. It pricked and smelled, close up, of some anti-septic used in cleaning. The darkness and silence seemed endless.

Actually both lasted just long enough for Patrick to pick himself up and race after the thug who had done this to us. He paused only to switch on the lamps and tell me to lock the doors. He himself closed them. I sat up, and felt mad.

I was mad because I'd been pushed like that from behind and because Patrick had gone off and left me. As two or three minutes ticked away I decided that his desertion made me madder than being pushed.

Then I started thinking of my clothes, specially about my hat, a costly John-Frederics item made of felt, flowers and ribbons which was now lying squashed under a table. I reached for it and examined it. The fact that it was not in the least damaged did not stop my feeling mad.

I was still sitting on the floor, getting madder every second, when the door opened and Patrick came in.

"Are you all right?" he asked, helping me up.

"Yes," I snapped back. Mad as could be.

He settled me into a chair. Tenderly. "You're sure you're all right darling?"

"Can't you see I'm mad? I'm perfectly furious. But I was madder while you were out of the room. I thought you'd gone off and left me the way you do sometimes and that I was missing something."

"You didn't," Patrick said. He took out his cigarettes and gave us lights. "The so-and-so got a couple of minutes' start. He'd vanished. This big place is so damned complicated. And I suddenly woke up to the fact that I didn't even know what he looked like. You should have locked the door while I was out, Jeanie."

"I didn't get around to it. I felt too mad. You ought to call the house detectives, or somebody."

"Huh-uh," Patrick said.

"Did I hurt your feelings, dear?"

"Why?"

"Suggesting we have the help of another detective?"

"Nope. Just don't want to get involved. After all, what do we know? We can't even describe the guy."

"Maybe he's got heavy black eyebrows and auburn hair."

"Maybe."

Patrick spied the slip of paper I had stooped to pick up in the entrance hall. He glanced at it and crumpled it into a ball and tossed it at a wastebasket. He sat down, with his long legs sprawling in front of him, on the foot of the satinwood bed.

"What was that, Pat?"

"Elizabeth Ashbrook phoned. I knew that. I'd already got the original chit in our box when I picked up the key."

"What time did she call?"

"The notice says five minutes past two. It's marked urgent. She wants to be called back."

"Don't do it, Pat!"

"Okay."

"But what would she want? At that hour?"

"I won't know unless I call her, Jean."

"Oh. Of course we must get involved. But it would be fun to know what she wanted. Did you notice the look on her face there at Brenda's when you said that man's name was von Osterholz? And her husband watched her. It was odd." I thought for a moment. "You know, I think I'd like Elizabeth Ashbrook."

"Do you?" Patrick said.

"I like her plain fascinating face and her funny hat. I like her long cigarette holder. With her it doesn't seem affected. Maybe that was she, calling again as we came in." Funny, the phone had rung only twice. "Maybe she realized how late it was and therefore hung up."

"Maybe. Only Liz, as they call her, didn't strike me as the kind to let a late hour stop her." Patrick got up suddenly and began searching the room, as if its elegant impersonality might hold some clue to explain the attack. "My God, Jeanie, I'm a hell of a detective. I didn't learn a thing from that business in the Park."

"It had no connection!" I declared. "That was engineered by Tony Konrad to get your hundred bucks. Hoping for more, of course."

"Huh-uh. It connects. I should have been on my guard. I should have looked out for you. I put you in a hell of a dangerous spot. If you had been hurt. . . ."

"I wasn't, except for my pride. What about you? The man jumped over me and went after you. I couldn't see in the dark with my face crowding the carpet."

Patrick reached up and touched the top of his head. "Ouch!" he said.

"Darling?"

He grinned. "It's not very serious. I haven't even got a headache. . . . Yes, I got conked! But why didn't he do a better job on me? It's pretty risky starting something in a hotel room. It's like that business in the Park—I mean, in both cases, a lot of risk was taken which added up to not very much."

I felt suddenly and utterly worn out with the whole thing.

"What does it mean?" I said. "We fall for a bid to Brenda Davison's rat-race. Afterwards we're tailed,—if Tony Konrad told us the truth. We're attacked in the Park. We get back to the hotel and Brenda is here waiting. Brenda tells a giddy yarn which is so tangled up with her inferiority complex, or whatever you call it, that it doesn't make sense. Pete Davison is hanging round. He was eyeing you before he ducked into that phone booth. And Elizabeth Davison Ashbrook has telephoned. We come up here. The phone rings again. Who was calling? You dive for it and before you get there we're both knocked down by—who?"

Patrick said, "If there's two of them that telephone call would be a swell device to distract my attention as I walked into the room. It would keep my back to the door."

"Pete Davison," I said, "ran for a booth the minute he saw you were on your way to the elevators."

"It would take perfect timing. I mean, to know when to call so that the phone would start ringing at precisely the right moment. I wonder if he's stopping in this hotel?"

"Easy to find out, isn't it?" I said.

"Why not?"

He started to the phone. There was a low firm knock on the hall door. My heart started jumping again.

Patrick stopped and turned to open the door. I followed him as far as the door from the entry, where he made me wait. He planted a foot against the door before opening it just wide enough to look out. Then he opened it wide.

Our visitor was a Mr. Evans, who was the uniformed guard we had met in the main corridor as we came to the room.

"I hope I'm not disturbing you," he said, speaking after entering and the door was closed, and even so in a very low tone. "A lady on this floor reported seeing a tall red-headed man in a gray suit running out of this corridor. She thought he had a gun in one hand. I met you and your wife as you came up tonight and I wondered if you had noticed anybody of that description?"

"We saw nobody," Patrick said, "except you, Mr. Evans."

"She probably dreamed it up," said Mr. Evans. "Sorry to have bothered you, Mr. Abbott." He bowed to me. "Sorry, Mrs. Abbott."

"You didn't bother us," I said. "I hope you catch the man."

Mr. Evans smiled. "I doubt if we will," he said. Meaning he thought there wasn't any. "Good night."

We said good night.

"Why didn't you tell him the truth?" I asked.

"I did. We didn't *see* the man, Jeanie." He started prowling around. "My God, I'm handed this case on a silver platter! Tony tails the guy and tells me what he looks like. A woman sees a red-head in a gray suit and reports it and a house detective passes it along to me. And here I am, dumb as they come. I've got no more idea what to do next than I had on my first case. I don't know how to proceed."

"Well, I do, Pat. Personally, I'm taking a bath. We're through with the detective business. Remember? We're getting out. We're buying a ranch and raising a family. I'm taking a bath, then I'm packing, and we're catching that nine o'clock plane."

"What about little Katy?" Patrick said.

"Katy?"

"She looked like such a sweet little kid, Jeanie."

"Darling, Katy was doomed to start with. What a family!"

The telephone rang.

Patrick dived for it. I looked on, feeling annoyed, getting mad. And with my heart pounding, too.

It was only Mr. Evans. The lady who had seen the red-head in the gray suit had retracted her statement. That is, she had not seen the gun really, the man merely had his hand in one pocket, and he might just have been just a man in a hurry, she said. Anybody might have a hand in his coat pocket.

"I thought you'd like to know, Mr. Abbott."

"Thanks, Mr. Evans," Patrick said. "Well, that's that," he said. He cradled the phone and reported what Evans had said.

He looked bitterly disappointed!

I went into the bathroom and undressed while my bath ran into the tub. I said to myself the hell with the Davisons. And I felt irritated when—sitting in my bath, all set to become rational the way a good long warm bath makes you—I could hear Patrick still prowling around. Now he was walking the carpet. Now he was leafing through a telephone book. I wondered if he would call Elizabeth Ashbrook. The hell with Elizabeth Ashbrook. Her problems were not our concern.

Of course, there were things I would like to know, such as why Katy was ill, and what the real lowdown was on Dr. Crossland's suicide. And what made Brenda tick, and what her ticking meant when she ticked. But I could get on without knowing, and very well.

The telephone rang.

Anxious not to miss anything I hopped out on the bath rug, thrust my feet in scuffs, wrapped myself in a big towel, and dashed out to listen.

"Yes, Mr. Couch," Patrick was saying, as I moved up and sat down beside him on the bed, to be close enough to listen in. "Yes, Brenda Davison did come here. Let's see—it's now 3:05. She left downstairs about 2:15."

"You're sure of the time, Mr. Abbott?"

"Yes. She looked at her watch and it reminded me to look at mine. It was 2:15."

"She was alone?"

"Yes. I understand a cab was waiting for her. She refused my offer to see her home."

Patrick didn't mention Pete Davison.

"Was she in evening dress?"

"Yes."

"I understand she came home after seeing you then," Mr. Couch said. "It seems she went home and changed her clothes. Anne Collier, who's staying with her just now, called me. She says Brenda came in and said good night to her—to Anne—and then went to her own room, presumably to go to bed. She was then in evening dress, so it must have been right after seeing you that she said good night to Anne. A short time later Anne, who had drowsed off, was wakened by the front door closing, downstairs. It's a big door, kind of noisy, which would be why it woke her. She got up and went to Brenda's room. Brenda was gone."

Patrick said, "It hasn't been very long . . ."

"I know. But there is a special reason why Brenda would not have gone out like that without telling Anne, Mr. Abbott. Anne is alarmed, and she ought to be. She called me to ask what to do. I am calling you because, as I said at the beginning of this conversation, Brenda consulted you professionally this evening. She told Anne, when she stopped in to say good night, that she had engaged your services. She didn't say why in particular, but we all know she has been very worried, and if there is anything you can do to make her easier in her mind, it's the thing for her to do."

"I see," Patrick said. "Can you meet me at Brenda Davison's apartment, Mr. Couch?"

"When?"

"Right away."

"Yes, of course. I have to dress. I live at some distance uptown. But I'll phone Anne to expect you, and I'll get there as fast as I can."

They said clipped good nights and Patrick hung up.

His eyes were shining green, the way they do when he gets genuinely going. My heart sank.

He remembered me, and reached for me and kissed me. The towel was hard to keep on.

"You smell nice, Jeanie," he said. "Now tuck in and I'll hop over to Brenda Davison's place and maybe I'll be back in half an hour with all the answers."

"No!" I said.

The telephone bell rang.

6

Elizabeth Ashbrook saved me from being forcibly tucked in bed. It was she on the phone, and while Patrick took the message I dropped my towel, and still damp in spots, fell into the clothes I had taken off, even the hat of ribbons, felt and flowers. I had no other anyway because we had expressed everything superfluous home.

Patrick cut Elizabeth off. She might have been thrust under a guillotine, so emphatic was her resistance when he said he could not talk any longer at this moment. "She's an imperious wench!" I thought. And her calling again, just then, in the middle of the crazy quilt of circumstance was just one item more. What did she want? Why did they need to call Patrick? New York was full of famous detectives. Nero Wolfe. Raymond Schindler. Really famous detectives.

In the hall, while we waited for the elevator, up walked Mr. Evans.

"Going out again?" he asked. My guilty heart gave a leap. Now we would have to tell him about that business in the room.

"Our last night here," Patrick said.

The detective grinned broadly. "Good old New York," he said. He eyed my hat. "Enjoy yourselves."

"That hat is worth a million," Patrick said, as we went down. "Nobody in her right mind would ever go any place serious in a hat like that. Promise me you'll always wear it."

"I hadn't time to find something sensible," I said.

"My God, I'm glad you didn't. That hat is perfect. It may even be worth what it cost. Nobody seeing that lid would ever even imagine we were . . ." In deference to the elevator man he shaped the last word with his lips only— "Sleuthing."

"Darling, don't be mean!"

"I'm not. I genuinely admire it. You, too. You're pretty wonderful, Jeanie."

"I seriously want to be useful," I said.

"You are," Patrick said. I looked at him straight, wondering if he really meant it.

Park Avenue at this hour was a boulevard to stroll along and enjoy. The haze had lifted again to the lofty rooftops. What cars there were moved gently and with symmetry and grace.

Then Tony Konrad appeared! My momentary delight in the scene took wing.

The black eyes glistened. The plump lips shaped their crescent smile.

"Hello, Bud," he said. "And Lady. Where to?"

Patrick headed for Tony's cab. I nudged him. In vain.

"Take us to 531 East 55th," he said. "Make it snappy, Tony."

Patrick looked at his watch as he slammed me into the cab. Tony started up and drove fast. Whenever he began to talk Patrick stopped him. We arrived at our destination with astonishing speed.

"Good," Patrick said, as we stopped. "He could have made it all right."

"Who could have made what?"

"Pete could have brought Brenda here and got back to the Waldorf by the time we saw him in the lobby."

Tony jumped out and held the door open. He seemed puzzled that Patrick was no longer in a grand rush.

"Don't you ever sleep?" I asked Tony.

"Yes, Lady. But not tonight. I took that dough Pat gave me to my wife. I had some supper and then I says I'll come back and hang around with the flag down because I've a hunch you'll need me."

"You must have wonderful hunches," I said.

"Yes, Lady. I seen that guy again, Pat. He come out of the hotel in a hurry just as I rolled up, after being home. I wondered should I phone you and then I thought maybe I oughtn't bother the lady."

Very kind of him, thought I. I felt stuffed. With suspicion.

"Which way did he go?" Patrick asked.

"He took the first cab in the rank and went north. I happen to know the driver so after a while he shows up again and I asks where he went and he says the guy gets out at York and 89th Street. Well, what good is that? Maybe he lives somewheres around there and maybe he don't. Maybe he grabbed another cab crosstown. If I'd've stuck around instead of running home a while maybe I'd've got him and could have tailed him to see what he'd do next."

Trying to sound smooth, which is not easy for a gal stuffed with dark suspicion, I asked, "Was he wearing the light-colored raincoat, Tony?"

"Yes, Lady."

The tall man who had followed us into our room had on a gray suit. Of course he could have parked the raincoat somewhere for the moment. Probably he would.

"Did he have red hair and a gray suit?"

"That I couldn't say, Lady."

We started into the apartment house.

"I'll stick around," Tony said.

"Well, keep well down the street then," Patrick advised. "You'd better not make yourself conspicuous, Tony."

There was no splendid doorman at this hour, and no one at the switchboard. The one elevator man stood yawning in front of the cages. He took no interest in us. He took us up in silence. He let us out, closed the grill, and went down.

Anne answered the bell almost at once. She said that Mr. Couch had phoned her to expect us. Lights were blazing in the hall, the little reception room opposite the entrance, the living room, on the stairs to the second floor.

"I didn't feel exactly safe," Anne said. She was wearing a cherry-colored padded silk robe and slippers. Her hair was braided in thick pigtails. "I wanted light. I'm a coward, frankly speaking," said she.

"We all are," Patrick said. "Where's Katy?"

"Asleep. I've got her locked in."

We stood in the hall. The light poured down on Anne's thick shining brown hair. Her eyes looked very black and her skin very white.

She was the kind of girl whose looks you liked better and better. Brenda swept you off your feet, but Anne started with being good-looking and arrived very soon by seeming very special, in looks and character too.

"Have you any idea where Brenda might be?" Patrick asked.

Anne shook her head. "I think Brenda was forced in some way to leave this house!"

"Why?"

Anne's hands spread out.

"She wouldn't leave of her own accord without telling me."

"You seem very confident?"

"Oh, yes."

"She told you she had talked to us tonight at the hotel?"

"Yes. I hadn't gone to sleep when she came home from dancing at the Plaza. That was the first time she came home. She seemed terribly worried. She said she simply had to have help. She was rather hysterical. She said she thought she might be murdered."

"Why?"

"Let's go up in Katy's sitting room so we'll be near her. Mr. Couch will be along soon, but the elevator men know him and will let him in and he will join us upstairs."

There was a private lift to the second floor but we walked up the wide easy stairs. The apartment without that crowd of drinkers and smokers looked very luxurious. There were deep green carpets, pale walls and iron railings. The architectural style was Italian Renaissance and the decorator had stayed with it. Everything had probably been selected by the decorator and that imposed a cold tidiness on the luxury. Still the place suited Brenda. A girl who could in 1492 have been a Botticelli model couldn't have been housed more becomingly.

Anne unlocked the door. We entered a room big enough to serve as the living room of a large family. It was Katy's private living room, or the day nursery.

All the lights were on. The furniture, aside from a few pieces for grown-ups, was nursery size. The chintzes were in a nursery pattern. Sofa and chairs planned for a little girl had slip-covers in a gay blue printed with smart little cream and black zebras. The draperies matched.

The walls were papered in a pale exquisite pink.

"Let's have a look first at Katy," Patrick said.

Anne went into an adjoining room and turned on a night lamp. The lovely child was sleeping serenely in her bed, her dark hair loose against her white pillow.

There was a studio couch which had been recently in use in the room.

"I slept there tonight," Anne said. "Usually Brenda stays at night with Katy, but tonight she said she would be late, so I slept on the couch. Before Katy was ill she slept alone in this room and the nurse used that one." She motioned at a door opposite the one from Katy's sitting room. "Nobody uses that now."

Patrick went over, tried the door, found it locked with the key in the lock. He unlocked it, stepped in, turned on the lights, looked around, came back and locked the door. It was a bedroom with an outlook on 55th Street. It did not share Katy's terrace.

Anne turned off the night lamp. We returned to the day nursery and closed the door.

In the nursery all doors and windows were locked with special locks and bolts. Patrick unlocked a French window and we stepped onto the terrace where we had seen Katy last afternoon.

The terrace lay in shadow. While Patrick checked the nooks behind tubs of boxwood and boxes of daffodils I examined the view. An old yellow moon was rising over the flat roofs and tall black stacks across the river. The hum of traffic on the bridge was hardly more than a purr.

The river itself was slightly covered with haze, but the water caught the moonlight in a dreamy way, and a tug hauling a chain of scows was curiously black and wavery against the vague surface.

Near-by a launch nuzzled the edge of the river.

Patrick came up beside me.

"Police boat," he said. I shivered, thinking of its chore.

We returned inside. He closed the window and bolted it.

What a life. What a sad thing are these locks and bolts for a little girl.

None of the furniture could accommodate Patrick's long legs. He sat on the floor. I chose an ottoman and Anne sat in one of two or three adult-sized chairs.

"How long will it take Couch to get here?" Patrick asked.

"Not too long, if he can get a cab," Anne said. "He lives a long way up, on Riverside. It was awful to get him out at this hour, but you have to. I mean, if Elizabeth Ashbrook had found out I had you over here without somebody she trusts present, like Mr. Couch, she'd have a fit."

"Is Elizabeth Ashbrook like that?" I asked.

"She can be," Anne said. She drew on her cigarette. "Usually she's rather swell, but she can be terrific. Liz has temperament."

"Did you call Pete Davison?" Patrick asked.

Anne flushed slightly. "Yes, I did. He wasn't in his room. Frankly, it's better to have Mr. Couch. Pete, strictly among ourselves, is faintly dim-witted."

"How come?" I asked.

"Oh, he won't listen. He's positively tainted with the notion that people ought to let each other alone. Normally, of course, that's so. But I doubt if Pete can get it through his thick head that Liz tortures Brenda. You'll think I'm exaggerating, because in some ways she's a peach, I mean Liz—but she's just too different. I'm sort of in between. I understand Brenda and to some extent maybe I understand Liz."

"Where is Pete staying?" I asked.

"Why, where you are."

I looked at Patrick. He was watching Anne.

Anne went on, intensely, "It's sabotage, in a way. Liz is driving Brenda crazy, and I doubt if she even knows it. Liz, I mean."

"Then it's not really sabotage," Patrick said, smiling. "Sabotage is deliberate, I believe."

"Maybe it is deliberate," Anne said. "That party you came to yesterday afternoon! Brenda did not ask half of those people, but surely that many wouldn't crash. You couldn't see the real guests for the phonies. It's happened before."

"Why?"

"Elizabeth Ashbrook wants Katy."

"Why would she go about it like that?"

"If it could be proved that Brenda wasn't the right kind of mother, Liz could take her. Because of the will."

"It's pretty hard to take a young child from its mother, Anne."

"Not when there's a will like the Davisons have to cotton to," Anne said. "I've never seen that will, of course, but apparently it takes care of everything. First it concentrates too much money on Katy, after which it specifies exactly how her parents and uncles and aunts are to behave." Anne sniffed with anger because of the will.

"Did you tell Pete the party was—sabotage?"

"Oh, not exactly. I complained a little. He was flip and said he'd seen even better parties in places like Reno, Nevada. He made me cross. Of course I couldn't out and out tell him Liz was trying to prove Brenda unfit to be Katy's mother so that she could get the kid—not to mention the use of Katy's income—but even if I did Pete wouldn't believe me. The trouble is he's never suspicious. You know what he said one day when I was telling him how depressed Brenda was? He said I ought to be writing those soap operas in which everybody always suffers." Anne sniffed again. "He slays me. He could swing the whole trick. If he would side with Brenda they would be two against Liz. But will he do it? No!"

Anne took time to get her breath.

"Pete likes sweet docile females," Anne said. "Can you imagine it? In this day and age."

I said, "I wonder, could Brenda have gone out again tonight with Pete?"

"Pete?" Anne said.

"They were dancing tonight at the Plaza."

There was a silence. Anne's lashes swept her flat cheeks. She fished in her pocket and brought out a smashed packet of cigarettes. She fumbled for a match. Patrick got up and gave her a light. She thanked him without looking at him.

I felt miserable. Brenda had lied to her then. Brenda hadn't told her she'd been out with Pete. I had been the one to tell her. I felt awful. I felt sorry and ashamed.

I couldn't even say I was ashamed because that would let Anne know that I knew she was hurt. She was trying to keep me from seeing it.

7

"God help you, Harold Couch," Elizabeth Ashbrook said, in her froggy voice, "if you've dragged us out at this hour for nothing."

We were gathered at the foot of the stairs in the lower hall of the duplex penthouse, where we had come when Mr. Couch had rung the bell a couple of minutes before. Mr. Couch had just been saying that he had had to ring, after all, because the new elevator man had refused to admit him, saying he didn't know him—which was certainly what the man should have done, he said. He was looking tired. He showed, when weary, that he was elderly, or almost, and no doubt he was tired of family squabbles and greed.

The arrival of Elizabeth and her hearty greeting put new life in him, in fact, in us all. She fascinated me. Her old hat might have been a dowdy contrivance to show off the interesting rugged face with the remarkable eyes. She carried no bag. I noticed that her minks were badly worn under the left arm. Her shoes were low-heeled, but also the only modish articles in her apparel.

She was leading a small black artfully-clipped French poodle, a species of canine which does not interest me very much but which, at that time, was very fashionable in New York.

Elizabeth's husband, Clive Ashbrook, would be a fashionable accompaniment to any woman. Slender, tall, dark, gracious and attentive, he immediately took charge of the group and without seeming effort managed to make us feel at ease. And in the kitchen, too, which Elizabeth declared, when Clive asked where we should sit, to be the only civilized room in the place.

"Brenda's place is too perfect," she said. "I've said so all along to Brenda herself. It's too fixed up. All the same, it suits her. The style of the apartment adorns her, and certainly she adorns it."

She spoke without malice. She showed no envy whatever of her young and exquisite sister-in-law.

Anne Collier had stayed upstairs to be near Katy. Patrick left us after we gathered in the kitchen to make a cursory search of the apartment. The Ashbrooks, Mr. Couch and I sat comfortably about the center kitchen table. Clive fetched Scotch and a syphon of soda and, oddly enough, he remembered that I had held a Manhattan glass in my hand when I came into the dining room in the afternoon, at the time the man was stricken, and asked if I should like one now. I declined, and was impressed by the delicacy of his memory and thoughtfulness.

"I only hope I *have* got you out for nothing, Liz," Mr. Couch answered

Elizabeth's croak. "Well, if we're all here when Brenda comes in it should teach her a lesson."

"Oh, let's not scold her," Clive said.

"Besides, it was a chance to walk the dog," said Elizabeth. "Hal, did you phone Pete?"

"Yes. He wasn't in his room."

A slightly shrewd expression came into Elizabeth's green eyes.

"You mean, he had checked out, don't you, Hal?"

Mr. Couch smiled gently. "I wasn't going to tell you, Liz."

"Well, why not? I warned you, didn't I?"

"I didn't believe you. I thought—I merely thought that Brenda was lonely and unhappy. Pete is a lot like Jack, especially since having his navy experience. It's made him seem years older. Jack was always old for his age and now that Pete is more settled the resemblance is striking."

"Pete's pretty nice," Liz said.

"So is Brenda," Clive said.

There wasn't so much as a flicker in her eyes as Elizabeth said, "Of course she is. But I didn't want it to happen, you know that. It's all wrong."

"I rather thought Pete was smitten with Anne Collier," Clive said.

"So did I," said Mr. Couch. "However . . ."

"Go ahead and say it. There is absolutely no use in our being so damn polite," said Elizabeth. "We all know that Pete needs money, and the Abbotts will have to know the truth if they're to handle this case." She looked at me and said, "Hal phoned us that Brenda had consulted your husband, though for the life of me I don't see quite how it all fits in. I mean, I would assume she went to see Mr. Abbott because of Katy. Being worried as she has been about the child."

"That was why she came," I said. I saw no harm in saying that, since it was partly why she had come.

"Well, if Brenda and Pete have eloped, what's to do, Hal?"

"We don't know that they have, dear," Clive said.

"Of course we don't," said Mr. Couch.

"Pete's incalculable," Elizabeth said. "He needs money badly. That ranch of his—you know he's taking big losses out there this year. After all, the temptation must have been pretty strong, even though Pete's heart wasn't in it exactly. Brenda's such a lovely-looking gal. And Brenda has money to burn. Davison money." Elizabeth laughed and fitted a cigarette into the holder, which she fished from her pocket. Her husband gave her a light.

Patrick returned, accepted a drink, and stood leaning against the magnificent sink.

"Did you find out anything?" Mr. Couch asked.

"Not a thing," Patrick said. "Brenda apparently took nothing, aside from what she walked out in. Anne thinks she left in a hurry, because she did not take the bag which belonged with her costume. The evening bag she used tonight is missing. Is there any place you know of where she might be likely to go?"

They looked at one another.

"In summer, yes," Mr. Couch said. "She's got a small place on Long Island. At Sands Point."

"But that's still closed up," Elizabeth said. "For the winter. There's no heat, no light, no phone."

"Exactly," Mr. Couch said.

"What about friends?" Patrick asked.

There was another exchange of glances, polished glances expert in admitting nothing.

Mr. Couch said, "I think Brenda has no real intimates."

"At least, we don't know them," said Elizabeth.

Clive said, "I think Hal is right about that, Liz. Brenda didn't pal around with anybody. I'm sure that the people she asks here are often people she hardly knows at all."

"That has worried us," said Mr. Couch. "Very much."

"Well, that's the way everybody carries on these days," said Liz. "You can't blame Brenda for doing what Clive and I would have done at her age. She's got the right to choose her own friends. Our real concern has been for Katy. We spoke to Brenda about her parties frankly. They tended to be extreme. And she stopped them after—after Katy was ill."

"She had one this afternoon," Patrick said. "Yesterday, rather. How do you explain that?"

"We don't," Elizabeth said. "Such people—and Brenda insisted that she didn't know half of them, but, after all, a cocktail party is a sort of free-for-all, and if she asks a number of people she doesn't know well they may fetch along others she doesn't know at all. So long as no damage was done it would not matter, except for Katy."

"What was Katy's illness?" Patrick asked.

The glances skimmed about, saying nothing.

"We don't know exactly," said Mr. Couch.

"It's a queer thing, an allergy or something," Elizabeth said. "Good Lord, how we miss Dr. Crossland, Hal."

"He'd been my doctor for thirty years," said Mr. Couch. "I do think this young Doctor Campbell who is carrying on his practice is first-rate. But he's not the same."

"About Brenda," Clive Ashbrook said. "What are we going to do?"

They all looked at Patrick. He said, "I suggest that you notify the police."

"Oh, no!" Elizabeth cried. The others agreed with her.

"Then I can suggest nothing," Patrick said. "If you are genuinely worried about her disappearance I don't think you could do better than to call the police. They've got everything to work with and the authority that goes with it."

All at once Elizabeth looked tired.

"Really!" she said. "We are not that worried. We are pretty sure that she and Pete have eloped, Mr. Abbott. Why don't we all go home and wait till morning? It's only two or three hours off now. If they've eloped what is there to do? Nothing. They are both of age. There is nothing in Father's will which forbids the widow of one of his sons from marrying the other son." Liz flicked an ash on the linoleum. "I wonder how he happened to overlook a possibility like that? Or maybe he would approve it. Perhaps you don't know it, Mr. Abbott, but the actions of this family are entirely directed by a man who is dead."

"Elizabeth!" Clive said.

"Well, it's true," Elizabeth said, and her statement was without vehemence or malice. "And it's unfair. I don't suppose people like Clive and me, who do nothing whatever, have any right to an easy income. But that is how we were brought up. We are helpless without it, and my father's will has cut us down until we—well, till we simply can't manage any longer." She laughed, and added lightly, "Let's go before I start crying on Patrick Abbott's shoulder, Clive."

She started to rise, and sat down again as Patrick said, "You would all benefit financially if Brenda died, I believe."

There was a stillness. Mr. Couch frowned.

Clive Ashbrook said, "That's rather a rugged way of putting it, Mr. Abbott."

"Rather," Mr. Couch agreed.

"Oh, don't be silly!" Elizabeth said. "It's true. If Brenda Davison were out of the picture the Davison money would again belong to the Davisons."

"And Katy?" Patrick asked. "Suppose Katy died?"

That was the closest Elizabeth came to showing nerves.

"We all adore Katy," she snapped out. "It would be a terrible thing to lose our little girl, even if it meant all the money in the world."

Mr. Couch said, "If you are not to work on the case, Mr. Abbott, I do think—well, I might say, you need not concern yourself with the details."

"Perhaps you're right," Patrick agreed.

"I think," Elizabeth cut in, "that he has a perfect right to ask us anything he likes, whether he works on the case, if it is a case, or doesn't. After all, we asked him here—or you did, Hal—and he's entitled to fair answers to any questions. Why not be honest? Brenda is an outsider. At the same time it is not her fault that she benefits at the expense of the rest of us by my father's will. It's just one of those things. He never met Brenda. The baby was born after he died. The will was purely and simply a device to deprive Clive and me of a proper share of the Davison money."

"It discriminated against your brothers as well as you, dear," Mr. Couch said.

"Not as much," Elizabeth said. "Either of them might have children, and as we well know all other grandchildren would share with Katy what is now entirely hers. Father knew when he made the will that I could never have children."

"We advised your father strongly against it," Mr. Couch said, gently. "You know that, Liz."

"Of course I know it, Hal. My father was an obstinate man. The hell with it! Why drag up the thing? But let's not call the police. Not yet, anyway. Let's not do anything at all until we're sure about Brenda and Pete."

"Jolly good idea," Clive said.

"Well, when we locate Pete—if we do—we'll know," said Mr. Couch.

"Pete will call us," Elizabeth said. She stood up and picked up the wrist-strap of the dog's leash. "Pete never keeps anything long to himself, Hal."

The men rose. Mr. Couch said, "Mr. Abbott is, of course, entitled to proper recompense . . ."

"Never mind that," Patrick said.

"Well, we're horribly grateful," Clive Ashbrook said, and I got the impression that his gratitude was slightly larger and more spontaneous, because there would be no charge.

"I've done nothing," Patrick said. "If I had, I assure you there would be a sizeable bill."

"Well, spoken," said Elizabeth. She looked at me and smiled. "Your hat is delightful. I wanted to say so this afternoon."

"Thank you," I said. "I should say it's not quite what a well-dressed detective should wear, but I like it."

She spoke to Mr. Couch. "Hal, is that your cab outside? Will you drop us?"

"Yes, it's mine," Mr. Couch said. Then she had not meant Tony Konrad's. "I can drop you all, I think. . . ."

"Never mind us," Patrick said. "We've got a cab waiting somewhere along the block. You'd better run on ahead. I'd like to check the doors and windows and talk with Anne again. Tell her what to do if anything happens."

"We're much indebted," Mr. Couch said. "If you want to make a charge,

Mr. Abbott, don't hesitate to do so."

"That's all right, Mr. Couch. It's been a pleasure. I'm as sold on young Katy as you are. I might suggest, however, that there should be servants living in this apartment, that is, if you are really worried on account of the child. Two young women like Brenda and Anne in a place of this size are not protection enough."

"Indeed, we agree," Mr. Couch said.

"We've heckled Brenda on that subject," Clive said. "Her present couple is perfect. They ought to live in, however."

"It needs only her say-so and they'll move in," Mr. Couch said. "I'll get after her first thing tomorrow—that is, if she hasn't gone away with Pete."

Elizabeth was suddenly irritable.

"Look, if Brenda has gone with Pete, what you're saying now is a waste of time. If she hasn't, we aren't to do anything anyhow till morning, so let's beat it. Good night, Abbotts."

"Good night."

When they had gone Patrick went up and talked with Anne a minute or two and then came down and looked up some addresses in a telephone book. Anne came down to put the chain on the front door after we were out. She would have to let the servants in, since the kitchen door was also chained at present. Patrick reminded her that if again alarmed she should call the police.

"Don't worry about what the family wants," he said. "Call the police if you're frightened. That's what they're for."

"All right," Anne promised. But her alarm seemed over. Like the others, she had mentally accepted the elopement as the explanation for Brenda's absence. If she felt sad or bitter, she did a good job of not showing it.

"I don't believe she's gone off with Pete," I said to Patrick, as we waited in the hall for the elevator to come up. "She wouldn't've eloped in a tweed suit she wears mornings on errands. She wouldn't've taken an evening bag with a tweed outfit like that. She was fussy about clothes, you could see that, even down to details like her nail polish. And Pete *is* keen about Anne. He doesn't like Brenda, not that way, anyhow. It's something else. They're all darned polite, but they resent Brenda. All they have to do is get rid of Brenda and they've got her money and the control of Katy's, too."

Patrick nodded in the direction of the ascending elevator.

"Shush!"

"Well, I don't think they got rid of anybody," I whispered.

Patrick said, "Even Anne accepts the elopement idea."

"Anne knows that Brenda knows she's in love with Pete. She thinks that's why Brenda would go off with Pete without telling her. I don't believe it.

That evening bag, with a tweed suit . . . Nope, she never would run away to be married dressed like that."

Outside, the night was ending. The darkness was opaque, but it was laced with the milky quality which precedes the dawn. In the country this hour is dramatic. Here, since for once there was nothing moving in the scene—until Tony started his engine and came to pick us up—the city seemed to lie in the sort of coma that precedes a handsome hangover.

We got into the cab.

Tony drove on around the block and headed in the direction of the Waldorf before reaching back a glove to Patrick. The glove had Brenda Davison's name in it, sewn in on one of those woven name-tapes. Tony said he had poked around while we were upstairs. He had searched the private boat-landing behind the apartment house. He had found this glove.

My suspicion rolled in. How did Tony know anything was up? Why was he doing all this? Patrick was asking it aloud. Tony replied that the elevator man had been so close-mouthed it roused his curiosity, so he had had a look around the place on his own and had found the glove. He said also that the servants' elevator at the rear of the house was open to anybody who knew how to operate it. Did Pat know that you could land a boat practically under the apartment house?

He dropped us at the Park Avenue entrance. Assuring him that we would need him no more tonight and advising him to go home and get some rest Patrick paid him off and we entered the hotel. In the foyer the rugs were rolled back. Cleaning women were at work and vacuum cleaners were droning. We walked through to Peacock Alley, skirted the lobby by way of the South Lounge, and arrived at the Lexington Avenue entrance. Outside again Patrick hailed a cruising cab. Not Tony's, for a change. The cab set us down about ten minutes later at 89th and York. We walked east for half a block and then down two steps into the vestibule of an old brownstone house made over into apartments. Patrick put his finger on the electric button under the nameplate of Paula Eastwood.

Her apartment would be on the first floor. One flight up. The superintendent of the building occupied the English-style basement.

There was no response. Patrick pressed the button again and again.

We stepped back out on the sidewalk. The early dawn now made all things gray, save for the mother-of-pearl river at the end of the street, and the thin pink line on the horizon through the great arch of Hellgate Bridge. A milk truck was trundling around the corner from Gracie Square. The milkman hopped out with a rack of bottles and ducked into the entrance of another brownstone apartment house.

Snatching my arm, Patrick marched me back into the vestibule and this time, instead of Paula Eastwood's bell, he tried that of the superintendent.

"He may think we're the milkman," he said.

"Don't bother to explain," I said bitterly. I added, "Anything."

The electric device which opened the inner door of the vestibule started buzzing. We entered the hall. Patrick trotted me up the flight of steps to the first floor.

Turning left at the landing we saw Paula Eastwood's door just ahead and on the right.

It was slightly open.

Patrick pushed it wider, very cautiously, and then stepped into the hall and found a light switch. Six feet away a heavy red plush curtain filled a doorway. The color of the plush was a dark bloody red which contrasted oddly with the cinnamon tint on the fingernails of the wax-white hand thrusting out under its hem.

8

Were I to choose the perfect setting for a fanatically brutal murder Paula Eastwood's parlor would have been it. Not that this notion came to me at the moment. I suspect I have no sang-froid. I wasn't having smart notions just at that time, because my whole mind was taken up with controlling my stomach.

"At last the body!" I should have been thinking. "Now we can go places!" I should have been saying to myself, as I stood staring at that white cinnamon-nailed hand.

Instead, I felt sick.

It was a dead hand. It was a bare hand. Its fortune in diamonds and sapphires was gone. So were the bracelets which had covered the small gauze pad which protected a burn on her wrist.

I stared at the hand as Patrick drew the curtain to one side of the door. The brass rings supporting the curtain made a flat clinking sound as they moved on the brass curtain-rod.

Then we saw the body.

Patrick flicked two wall switches and the room went brilliant with the light from an old-fashioned chandelier and several lamps. The naked body looked vividly white as it lay face-down on the red-patterned carpet.

Face-down? It had no face! The head lay crushed against an ugly slimy black-red splotch which shaped a crude circle around the pale coronet of hair. There was blood in the hair.

I felt weak, and Patrick elbowed me to a chair. "Don't look at it," he said. He closed the outside door and made a quick turn through the apartment. He was back in a flash and started cursing with rage as he stooped to examine the body.

To avoid looking at the body I sat stiffly on my straight chair and looked at the room. It was tremendously over-furnished and over-curtained. That curtain in the door, under which Brenda's hand had shown snow-white, was non-essential. The carpet was not really a carpet, but a collection of oriental rugs, so profuse they overlapped each other. A greedy woman, this Paula Eastwood. She liked too-muchness. She liked the crudely ornate. French dolls sat on the red-plush sofa. There were fancy tufted rayon-velvet cushions and ruffled rayon lampshades. She loved that dark bloody red. Every way you looked there was red.

The air itself smelled of all these fabrics, and like bananas. There was a bowl of them, I discovered later, in the kitchen.

"What shall we do?" I asked. Patrick did not answer. I bucked up and watched him examine the body. The arm was limp. Rigor mortis had not set in. Dead then less than two hours, which checked with the time she'd left her apartment. The waistline was even slimmer than you'd think, the hips somewhat heavier. There was a great welt, Patrick said, at the base of the skull, under the pale blood-stained hair.

The face was a mass of red pulp. Beneath it was a blood-sodden towel, which had been used to cover the face while it was being beaten to destroy the identity of Brenda Davison.

The bludgeon had been an andiron. Carelessly smeared, it was back in the fireplace, where it nested among coy frills of red and gold crepe-paper which Paula Eastwood evidently thought prettier than a laid fire.

I watched Patrick, peering at everything, touching nothing. He was wearing gloves, but he never did do any unnecessary handling.

"How are we going to explain being here?" I asked then.

"Maybe we won't have to."

"Darling! Of course we will. Which reminds me, how do we happen to be here?"

"Routine."

"You'll have to explain it to me, Pat."

"Please don't talk. We've got to get out of here before the milkman shows up."

"Why?"

"The murder has to be discovered and reported to the police. The sooner the better, so he's a good bet. The murderer wanted the body discovered, I think. That's why the hall door was left open."

"Maybe he was in a hurry and forgot to shut it?"

"Maybe. Don't prattle, please."

"Why can't we report it?"

"And get bogged down in official red tape?"

"But we'll have to say we were here. It wouldn't be honest. . . ."

"In due time. Kindly shut up. Now, come along, and let's have another quick-see around this dump."

"Dump is right," I said.

Back of the parlor—or the murder-room if you prefer—was a bedroom. It was also crowded with things. There was an ornate mahogany bed inset with huge blobs of circassion walnut. A highly imaginative rose-rayon coverlet, appliquéd with green and red flowers, covered the bed. Rose brocades and coarse lace draped the windows and dressing table. An ankle-deep rose rayon carpet covered the floor. What a contrast to the coldly perfect Renaissance-decked-out penthouse where Brenda had lived! Perhaps she preferred something like this. Left to herself, away from a decorator, maybe this would have been her choice.

Patrick ducked down and picked up something almost hidden by the ruffles of the coverlet. It was a glove, with Brenda's name-tape in it, possibly the mate to the one handed us by Tony Konrad.

He scrutinized it, and left it where he had found it. It was the only object belonging to Brenda that we found in the place. There was not time to go over the garments crushed together by their profusion in the clothes closet, but nothing of Brenda's showed up in our cursory inspection except the glove.

"He didn't mean she should be identified," I said. "But that glove does it. Poor thing. Poor Brenda."

Patrick said, "Now for the rest of the place, and get a move on."

There was a bath behind the bedroom. The bath opened into a short hall. At the rear of the apartment was the kitchen. Patrick flicked the kitchen lights on and off and turned back through the hall into another room. It was a beauty shop. It gleamed with fine gadgets and cabinets. Driers and waving machines stood about. Glass-fronted cases held hair tints, glosses, nail enamels and lotions.

"She must be a beauty operator with a private clientele," I said. "What will she think when she comes in?"

"Maybe she won't come in," Patrick said, studying a case of nail enamels.

"You mean she's an accomplice? How horrible! I suppose she lives here. I suppose she owns all those things. Those French dolls, and those lamp-shades, that bed, all those fancy clothes packing the closet."

"Somebody owns them," Patrick said. "And I don't think it's von Osterholz."

"Oh?"

Patrick was bending his eyes close to one bottle of nail polish. I said, "So that's why we came. Tony told you the man in the raincoat got out of his friend's taxi at 89th and York."

"So he did," Patrick said, his gaze hard on the nail polish.

"You don't trust Tony entirely, Pat?"

"I don't trust anybody entirely, except you."

"Not even me. You never tell me everything, straight off."

"I do eventually," Patrick said. He moved over to another cabinet filled with bottles.

I said, "You knew all along that Tony's tailing us like that was fishy. It doesn't happen like that—in New York. How often have I said that tonight?"

"Pretty often," Patrick said.

"You knew he was dangerous. That's why you ditched him at the Waldorf. That's why you got another cab to drive us up here."

"Just common sense. Tony's too nosy. If he doesn't look out somebody will polish him off one of these days." He lifted his head. "Shush!"

He stood listening. His ears are better than mine. I heard nothing till the doorbell rang.

It was a buzzer, and located in this room. It sounded positively venomous and determined. It intended to be answered, and no mistake. Patrick turned off the lights in the shop. We stood close together, listening.

"Paula Eastwood maybe," I said.

"Maybe."

"Did you lock the front door?"

"No. I closed it. I don't know if the night lock was on, or wasn't. Damn careless of me, too."

"What shall we do?"

I knew that Patrick grinned. He put his arm around me and whispered, "Hope."

"Is there any other way out?"

"Back door in the kitchen. Heaven knows what it leads to. Your husband is a dimwit, Jeanie. I had only one plan, to step lively and scram before the milkman got to this house."

"The milkman came sooner than you thought, that's all."

"I don't think it's the milkman, unless he gives our friend Paula a pretty special service. . . ."

"Maybe it's the police?"

The buzzer abruptly ceased. The silence was lovely. But only for seconds. Whoever it was began to pound on the door.

"I guess it's locked, Pat."

"Yes. But we've got to get out some other way. Pronto."

"But how?"

"There's only the back door. We can try it."

We slipped into the little hall and went into the kitchen. Through the windows the daylight outside showed darkly on tight clusters of the heaven-trees which are everywhere in New York gardens. I followed Patrick out the door and down some steps. It seemed like walking into a trap. The garden was walled by a high broad fence. The boards were perpendicular and hard to scale. Even so you would only climb over into another fenced-in garden.

My mind darted to my nylons as I measured that fence. I even thought of my hat! A woman is an idiot to buy such a hat. Serves me right, I thought. I ought to get rid of the hat. But where? How? Somebody would find it, and it would be easy to trace.

Patrick was holding me by one hand as he moved cautiously toward the lighted windows of the basement kitchen. The superintendent's kitchen, and there was no one in it at the moment. Patrick tried the door. It opened. I followed him into the small clean modern kitchen. The kettle was boiling on the stove. Coffee was perking in a white-enamel pot.

I quaked. I felt like a thief, a heel, a criminal.

A door stood open into a short hall. Through another we could see a bathroom which must open at the other end into a bedroom or living room. I imagined the superintendent's wife, throwing on something, getting ready to come out and finish getting breakfast. We might walk into her, face to face. She would scream. We would have to explain our presence, and no one would believe us.

Patrick led me toward the hall door. At the end of the hall another door opened into the main hall. We stood in the hall and saw the milkman trot down the two steps from the sidewalk carrying a basket of quart bottles of milk in one hand and in the other a second filled with pint bottles and half-pints of cream. He put his thumb on the superintendent's bell. He waited.

Upstairs a woman let out a wild scream.

Grasping my arm firmly Patrick walked straight to the door and admitted the milkman. The man rushed past us with only one glance, and that at my hat. We walked out the front door into free air.

In the street the morning light was clearer than in the tree-arched back garden. To the east the vast arch of the bridge spanning the meeting waters at the end of the street stood against a rosy sky. The water danced in the new-born daylight. A breeze had come up and the air smelled sweetly of spring.

We started to walk in the direction of the river, walking fast but careful to avoid too much haste.

A taxicab parked near the corner started its motor. It slid up beside us. The driver reached back and opened the door. I was inside and Patrick was with me before I saw that our driver was Tony Konrad.

9

I reached out for the telephone and withdrew my hand, hoping that Patrick would answer it, thinking suddenly of what had happened when we left Paula Eastwood's apartment. I had wanted to get out of the cab the minute I saw who was driving it, but Patrick merely told Tony Konrad the Waldorf and to make it snappy. Tony Konrad was hurt. He asked through the open panel behind the driver's seat why we had given him the doublecross like that. Patrick did not answer.

"I saw you," Tony said then. "I had to drive around the block to get back in the rank and I saw you take the other cab. I tailed you. I almost lost you. Just by chance I saw you come out of that place on 89th Street and then go right back in again, so I stuck around, thinking you might want me."

Patrick asked Tony why on earth he thought we should want him and Tony said then that the elevator man at Brenda Davison's had acted queer. "He asked me if you was a detective and what went on," Tony said.

I thought he was making it up. It had seemed to me that the new night elevator man took no interest in us or in anything.

Patrick told Tony he was sticking his neck out, horning in on everything like that. Tony said plaintively that it was his own neck. Patrick said that his good wife Bertha and his kids and grandkids had an interest in it. In the talk which Tony kept going till we reached the hotel there was nothing of any importance and yet, in my opinion, much that was sinister. By what magic did he keep bobbing up like this? Why? The day had turned gray again as soon as we left the river and moved through deep streets, and about us there were sights and shadows which one could without exaggeration call sinister, but to me the most sinister of all was the plump raggedy bright-eyed omniscient Tony Konrad.

The telephone bell kept ringing.

I wakened enough to hear the shower-bath humming beyond the half-opened door of the bathroom. I reached for the phone and said, "Yes?"

Peter Davison said, "May I speak to Patrick Abbott?"

"He's in the shower," I said, yawning.

"Oh, Mrs. Abbott?" He was on very good behavior. "Pete Davison speaking. I'm sorry to disturb you, but I've got to see Pat. I've got to. It's a matter of life and death."

Death. I saw the white body, the faceless face. I shuddered. Suddenly I was very wide awake.

Oh, my goodness! This was important! This was the missing Pete!

"I don't like to say what's on my mind over the phone, Mrs. Abbott."

"I'll call him, Mr. Davison."

I hopped out of bed and ran to fish Pat out of his bath. When he heard it was Pete Davison, he came to the phone dripping, half-draped in a towel. His dark hair was plastered down wet. Water rolled down his face from his eyelashes and his long thin hairy legs looked very wet. I laughed because he looked funny. When he tried to light a cigarette water drowned it so I dried his face with a tissue and lit one for him, a favor on my part because I don't like the taste of tobacco before breakfast. Meanwhile he kept the receiver clamped to one ear.

"You're here in the hotel, Pete? What's your room number?" Pete answered something and Patrick said, "You're just around the corner from us, so why don't you pop over here? Sure. . . . Pronto."

"My goodness!" I said. I moved fast, washing my face and brushing my teeth, getting into the light-weight tie-silk robe I carry when we travel by air, puffing up the pillows and smoothing the covers and then getting back into bed. Patrick toweled himself and brushed his hair and was in another tie-silk robe—it did not match mine, being years older and anyway Patrick won't stand for that matching business—when Pete tapped on the door. Patrick admitted him.

The woman had told the house detective that a red-haired man in a gray suit had gone running along our corridor.

Pete Davison had on a gray suit. Definitely, his nutmeg hair would be called red. His room was on this floor, just around the corner.

Patrick gave him a chair and then opened the blinds. It was broad daylight outside. The sun was shining. I glanced at the traveling clock by the telephone. Ten minutes past eight. It was close to six when we'd got to bed. I hadn't been sleepy. I'd never expected to sleep again, but I had.

I said, "Have you had breakfast, Pete?"

He shook his head. He seemed in a daze.

Patrick said, coming back from the windows, "Call room service, Jeanie. Pete, what will you eat?"

"Nothing," Pete said. Patrick said, to me, "Order orange juice and toast and plenty of coffee for three. And bacon and eggs, plenty of them, and tell them to step on it. Cigarette, Pete?" Looking definitely dazed, Peter Davison took the cigarette. He started smoking the cigarette before he said to Patrick, "I saw you come in last night. I wanted to talk to you then. I even went into a telephone booth and asked for your room. I heard your phone buzz. Then I got cold feet and hung up."

"That's too bad," Patrick said. Pat doesn't believe him, I thought. He was sitting on one corner of the foot of the bed, so that I saw him in profile. He had shaved, so he must have been up for some time. Maybe he hadn't slept. Maybe he'd been out while I slept. Maybe I had missed something.

"I've no right to take your time, Pat."

"Why not?" Patrick's voice was a little sharp.

Pat knows something, I thought. He knows something I don't know about Pete. But did he really telephone our room or did he merely take the next elevator up after us? A red-headed man in a gray suit.

Yet to look at Pete Davison, and go on being suspicious, was impossible. His gay gray-eyed face was already getting bright and confident. His hair seemed crisper. His eyes were beginning to shine.

"I've got no right to ask your advice, because I've got nothing to go on. Nothing but my lousy imagination. And maybe that's nuts. Maybe I've been away from this so-called civilized life so long that I've lost my touch. Maybe what I think's cockeyed."

Patrick said, "No harm in airing your imaginary troubles here, Pete. They'll go no further, anyhow."

Again I had that ugly creepy darkness of the mind, as if what Pete was about to tell us was a thing I'd rather not know.

Pete ground out the half-finished cigarette and leaned forward, his hands clasped, his fingers working.

"Okay, here goes. But remember, I can't prove anything. I'm only suspicious. Something is wrong in the family set-up and I can't figure out what. They're all nice people. Maybe Clive and Elizabeth aren't exactly up my alley, and maybe Brenda isn't my ideal girl, but so what?"

Isn't? Didn't he know that Brenda was dead? Who knew that yet? The woman who screamed. The superintendent. The milkman. The police. And the murderer.

"Well, my feelings about the whole bunch got so hard to live with that I decided to scram and forget it. It's the kid, Katy. I hate seeing her grow up in such a mess. So I checked out of this hotel and tried to plane out but couldn't get a seat, so I dashed down to Grand Central meaning to take the first train."

"What time was this?"

"It was after you came in last night. Right after I started to phone you, and didn't."

"Some time around two-thirty, then?"

"Yep. I never noticed the time. I went up and got my bag and left. I got a taxi to Grand Central on the Lexington side and got to the station just in time to miss a through Chicago train. So I had to wait around a while. It was pretty dreary in the station so, after a while, when a train was called which wasn't so fast I decided to get on it and get off later and pick up a through train somewhere up the line."

"You didn't have a reservation?"

"Nope. Couldn't get one. Had to ride the coach. Well, I got on this train . . ."

"What time was that?"

Pete rubbed a rugged check. "My God, I don't know! Some time between three and four, I guess. What difference?"

"Never mind. Go on."

"There's no need dragging it out, Pat. The minute I sat down on that train and it started moving through the tunnel I started feeling like a first-class heel. If I'd had any guts I'd've left it at 125th Street. Instead, I sat like a lump and rode on and on. It started getting daylight. There was a haze over the Hudson and the tops of the Palisades looked like gold. The prettier the country got the worse I felt. Finally the train started slowing down for a station and I grabbed my coat and got off."

"Where was that?"

"Hell if I know. When I got on the platform I saw by the signals that a train was due for New York, so I crossed the tracks and when it pulled in a minute later I got on it. Milk train, I guess. Stopped at every cross-roads."

"What time did you get back to Grand Central?"

"I don't know. I got off and had to wait maybe ten minutes for a cab. I got back here, checked in, got the same room, of all things, and then called you. That's the story. For whatever it's worth. I wasted time acting like that and I'm wasting more telling it, I guess."

"Just why did you come on to New York now, Pete?"

Peter Davison gave Pat a long level look before he answered.

"To raise money. Fat chance I had."

"Why not?"

"The estate is entailed. I knew that, but somehow I got the idea that I could snag Hal Couch into letting me sell out my share, or part of it, or something. Not a chance. My father knew what he was doing when he appointed Hal to sit on his money-bags. Of course, Liz has been trying the same thing all along. She—well, that's her business." He said then, "Liz has a bad heart. She jokes about it when she has to refer to it, which is plenty seldom, but she's got it so she'd like to have her share of the estate and spend it now on Clive."

"Do you like Ashbrook?"

"Sure, I like him. But the money's Elizabeth's, see."

Patrick said, "You were out with Brenda last night, weren't you, Pete?"

Pete nodded. "You saw us, didn't you? At the Plaza?"

"We saw you when we first got there. Where did you go then?"

"We went along to the Stork Club, stayed there about an hour, and then I took Brenda home."

"What time was that?"

"Oh, some time before two o'clock. I didn't notice. I was already thinking about beating it. I dropped her at her place and walked back to the Waldorf."

"Walked back?" I said.

"Sure," Pete said. "I thought a walk would straighten me out. I was sorry I had to see that place she lives in again. I get to thinking about Katy, penned up up there. Good God! But that's what I want to talk to you about." His eyes blazed. "That's the problem."

I was thinking, why didn't Patrick come out with it? Why didn't he ask Pete if he could make his alibi good when the police started investigating Brenda's murder?

But how could he? Presumably we didn't know yet that she was dead.

Patrick asked, "What happened then?"

"You mean, after I left Brenda? Well, I walked back and stopped in a hamburger joint and got a sandwich and some coffee to settle the fancy fare I'd been wolfing with the liquor all evening. Then I came back here. Just after walking in I saw you at the desk, getting your key."

"Why didn't you speak to me then? Instead of phoning?"

Pete looked at me. "To be frank, I wanted to speak to you alone. I didn't want to spill the dirt before Jean."

"You haven't spilled any yet," I said.

Patrick said, "You took Brenda home twice last night, didn't you, Pete?"

"Twice? Not unless I was drunk and don't remember it. I took her home after we left the Stork Club. The evening was her idea, by the way. I had a date with Anne. She broke it, and then Brenda phoned and having nothing else to do I took her on the town—oh, forget it. I don't care much for that sort of thing. Maybe I've turned into a hick, with no taste any more for the night life. Brenda had a good time. She doesn't have much fun, if you ask me, and it was only a few hours out of my young life, so what."

Patrick asked, "Anne broke your date so that you could take Brenda out?"

Pete said, "Something like that. Then Brenda happened along. If Brenda hadn't shown up I doubt if I would have left New York. The way she goes on—the—well—the way she—talks . . ."

"Let's have it, Pete."

"All right. I think she's crazy."

Patrick asked, "Did she drink much last night?"

"Hardly at all. She seldom either drinks or smokes."

"Was she always confused in her thinking?"

Pete said, "To tell the truth, when I came East was the first time I ever met Brenda. But I think she can be all right. Get her out of this town, away from Liz and Clive, and she'll snap out of it, I think."

"You think they do something to her?"

"I damn well know they do! And what's the point? Their kind is finished, I hope."

"How do you mean?"

"They're useless people. They're no good. Yet they've got Brenda all mixed up trying to be somebody she's not."

"Would either of them commit a crime? To get something they wanted badly?"

Pete's mouth opened. "My God! How do I know? See here, I've got nothing against Liz and Clive personally. It's their type I don't like."

"What's your interest in Brenda's set-up, Pete? I know you're related to her by marriage, but what else?" Pete just stared. "Have you asked her to marry you?"

Peter turned a dull red which did not become his nutmeg thatch.

"That's none of your damn business!"

"Maybe not," Patrick said.

"Only, why did you ask?"

"I'm trying to get things straight. I'm sorry if I embarrassed you, Pete."

"Damn well you did!" Pete said.

A waiter tapped on the door and came in wheeling a cart with our breakfast. He arranged the table so that I could breakfast in bed and drew up straight chairs for the men. By the time he had set out the service to his personal satisfaction and had faded out the door Pete Davison had cooled off.

"I'm sorry I got so mad," he said.

"I'm glad you did," Patrick said.

"I talk too much. I know it. That's why I came to you. I figure I'd better do my talking from now on to somebody who can do something about it. I came East strictly to raise money and to visit the family on the side. I got out of the navy last November to find my ranch all shot. I had a crooked foreman, for one thing, and—well, never mind all that, I was in a hole. I still am. I need money. I don't want to borrow, if I can help it, and I had some sort of screwy notion that if I came here and talked to Hal Couch and Liz and Brenda I could lay hands on some of my capital and do a few things I was planning to do on the ranch when the war struck. Then I saw that kid." His voice softened. "She's the spitting image of my mother. I don't remember many things about my mother, but her face has always stayed with me, and here is this little girl, exactly like her." For a moment Pete was silent. "There is Brenda, scared to death of something, afraid even to employ a proper nurse. There's Anne, who ought to be—well, not doing that. So I suggested taking Katy out West. Brenda, too, of course. My ideas might have been a bomb. Oh, they didn't exactly blow up. There wasn't any noise, but nobody seconded the motion."

He was hungry. He applied himself to the food. I didn't want my eggs and bacon, so Pete dispatched them as well as half of my toast.

"Did you know that Brenda consulted me last night?" Patrick asked then.

Up went Pete's eyebrows.

"She did? When?"

"After you took her home. She came back here and waited for us to come in."

Pete frowned. "Why?"

"She seemed worried about the child. Just as you are."

"I'm not really worried," Pete corrected him. "I'm disgusted. I think that's a hell of a set-up for any kid."

"Brenda thinks that an attempt was made a couple of months ago to murder the child."

"Did she tell you that?"

"More or less. She asked me to try to find out what it was all about. She was pretty vague. She told us that all kinds of people came to that party yesterday who weren't invited. She thinks that sort of thing is planned to show that she is not a suitable mother for Katy, so that one of you Davisons, you or Elizabeth, can take over the child and her income."

Pete sat up, a cup of coffee poised in the air.

"The woman is nuts!" he said.

"Why?"

"What would I do with Katy with nobody to take care of her? What would Liz do with the kid? Liz has that heart."

"Are you sure?"

Pete turned red again and said primly, "See here! Whatever else you may think of Liz, she's honest."

"She needs money, doesn't she?"

"Oh, sure. But . . ."

"Maybe she genuinely thinks Brenda unfit to have charge of Katy."

"Brenda's her mother. Liz couldn't take her from her mother without a fight, and she wouldn't try. It never occurred to me that anybody would try to separate them, Pat. Unless Brenda is really insane."

"What about Ashbrook?" Patrick asked.

"What about him?"

"He strikes me as a very smooth number, frankly speaking."

"Maybe he is. But I can't see Clive playing daddy to a three-year-old kid."

"What other way is there?"

Pete thought it over. "There isn't any other way."

Patrick said, "How exactly do you think I can help you, Pete?"

Pete said, "How about talking Brenda into seeing things my way? I've got a big comfortable place, which will be ideal for the kid to start with, and Brenda can later on get them fixed up in Tucson or Phoenix or some place like that. If she prefers to live in town. It's a good life. They'll like it. I want them to go west with me."

"In that case, you'd have some say about the spending of Katy's money, wouldn't you? Whether you did or didn't marry Brenda?"

Pete set down his cup.

"You go to hell!" he said.

Patrick grinned. "You win," he said. "But I doubt if I could be any use. Why not see a lawyer?"

"Too slow. Besides, all I want is someone to talk sense to Brenda. It's a job for a guy who can make people realize what they ought to do. From what I've heard about you, you're it."

It was too late. The image of the dead woman rose up and a flood of confusion filled my mind. While I wondered how Patrick could sit there poker-faced, Clive Ashbrook telephoned. He wished to talk with Patrick. I handed the phone over without saying who was calling. Now what?

My heart was pounding like mad.

"Good God!" Patrick said. His tone could almost convince me that he was shocked with horror and surprise. "You say you identified her?" Ashbrook evidently said he had. "Your wife, too?" Ashbrook said that his wife wasn't up to it. "Pete happens to be here with us," Patrick said then. He handed Pete the phone. He moved away a little and stood watching him closely.

"My God Almighty!" Pete said. Then he said, "Well, if I have to have an alibi I'll have one. That's my business, not yours. What about Anne?" He listened, and then said, "I'm going over there now, even if I have to mow down policemen, understand?" He listened, and squirmed, and then said, "That's a hell of a note. Good-bye."

He cradled the receiver.

"I've been wasting your time," he said. He started toward the door, and stopped, and said, "I guess this is really in your line, Pat."

"You can count on me," Patrick said. "Run along now and look after your girl. I'll see you both later."

10

Lieutenant-Detective Jeffrey Dorn took his round sky-blue eyes off my hat. For goodness' sakes, I thought. If ever I get a minute, that is, if there is ever one minute during which I may not miss something, I'll get myself another hat.

The police detective said, "Unless Peter Davison can prove his story of what he did between 2:45 and 7 this morning we'll have to arrest him. At the moment I'm giving him a little rope."

"Where is he now?" Patrick asked.

"He asked to go up and see the child. One of our men is with him."

I shivered, and a hollow shaped itself in my heart. Peter Davison was not likely to be discreet. Probably he couldn't.

Patrick showed only indifference. We were sitting in Brenda's drawing room. The Italian chairs were pale oak upholstered in yellow velvet brocade. The drapes were the same pale yellow. The carpet was a deep mossy green. The table in front of the lieutenant and his stenographer and the coffee table before the sofa where Patrick and I sat and the long refectory table by the French windows were apparently Italian antiques. I hadn't noticed these details yesterday afternoon because there were too many people.

The room was very beautiful, but, in my opinion, unlivable because there was no place in it where you could settle down and relax. The great hooded fireplace seemed like an ornament, and I wondered if a match ever was put to the huge assortment of kindling and neat logs. There was a portrait of Brenda between two windows overlooking the terrace. The artist had caught the glade look.

"She doesn't look much like that now," Dorn said in his emotionless way when he caught me looking at the portrait.

"Peter Davison was among the last to see Brenda Davison alive," Dorn said. "He admits having spent the evening with her, however. He say he brought her home—here—some time around two A.M. We can check that, I think. He let his cab go here and walked back to the Waldorf, he says. On the way he had a hamburger and coffee. Back at the hotel he says he fiddled around a while with the idea of leaving town, and then got his bag, checked out, and took a cab to Grand Central." He paused, and then said, in the same matter-of-fact tone. "It seems to me that Davison, if contemplating a journey all the way to Arizona, would at least go to the trouble of verifying train schedules before going to the station. Specially the way transportation is now. He didn't, according to his own story. He drove down to the station and—having just missed a through Chicago train—he waited around until a slower train was announced—one which makes a good many stops, and goes only as far as Buffalo. Suddenly, an hour or more out of New York—he doesn't know how long exactly—he gets off the Buffalo train and takes another train back to New York. He even claims he doesn't know where he changed trains."

"Maybe a conductor or somebody will remember him," I said.

"The period of time we're most interested in is that he says he spent in Grand Central Station, Mrs. Abbott. He thinks he was there about an hour. During that hour, according to the medical evidence, Brenda Davison was murdered."

"You can be that certain about the time, Dorn?"

"It could have happened a bit earlier or a bit later. The point is, who will swear that Peter Davison spent that hour in Grand Central Station?"

"I would," I said.

Dorn stared at me. "You saw him during this time?"

"Of course not. I just think he tells the truth."

"I'm afraid that isn't enough, Mrs. Abbott," said the detective. Not with patience. "I might add that that Davison's smart-aleck ways don't help him, either."

"Oh, he's just fresh," I said. "I have a friend in New Mexico who says that boys who don't whistle after girls at least once in their life don't ever amount to much."

"Really," remarked the detective. My goodness, I thought. Dorn never had whistled at anybody. Ever. What a *faux pas*!

"Oh, dear. I don't suppose anybody ever remembers anybody they see in Grand Central Station."

"Of course not," Dorn said, poisonously.

"If he'd only got a reservation!" I said.

"That's his bad luck," Dorn said.

My goodness! The police detective was just as set in his ideas as he was two years ago, when he had made up his mind that Ellen Rawlings had killed that heel who was then her husband.* And he didn't look like a police detective at all. He looked like a successful business man. There was gray now in his fair hair, but there were no lines in his round angelic face, not even about the round blue eyes. He was carefully dressed in a gray suit, a blue shirt, and there was blue in his necktie. His shoes were black and neatly polished.

"The others tell plausible stories," Dorn said. "The Ashbrooks were in their suite at the St. Regis. Anne Collier was here in the apartment with the little girl. Of course she could have gone out and come back in, but Anne Collier had no reason to murder Brenda Davison. Unless she was jealous.

There is that possibility. The Ashbrooks and Peter Davison would benefit financially from Brenda Davison's death. They admit that. The Ashbrooks also admit not liking her very much. Or rather, Mrs. Ashbrook does. Peter Davison seems to have liked her well enough to take her around the night spots. Maybe he was working himself up for the kill. He was desperately in need of money. He says so. That is why he came East."

"He'd better get a lawyer," Patrick said.

"Says he won't," Dorn said. "He's a very stubborn young man."

"Oh, he's in love!" I said.

Patrick's sidelong glance was practically a nudge. But it came too late.

The lieutenant eyed me. "A good deal of nonsense goes on under the name of love, Mrs. Abbott. It isn't an excuse to murder and never has been."

"It's an excuse to run out of town and then run right back again."

"Not in this case, Mrs. Abbott."

"I don't agree!" I said.

"Who's he in love with?"

I did not answer. I realized suddenly what I had done. I felt wretched. But the damage was done.

Then he said, "If it's Miss Collier, she seems a reasonable sort. However, as I just said, we're keeping an eye on her. The jealousy motive. But I think that's pretty far-fetched. Of the four—the two Ashbrooks, Davison and Miss Collier, I'd mark her off the list first."

Lieutenant Dorn didn't give a hoot anyway for my ideas. As if purposely to exclude me, he turned to Patrick and said, "How come you're in on this?"

"Haven't the Davisons told you?"

"They have. I want your own statement."

"Brenda Davison had heard of me through Anne Collier, it seems. Anne's a friend of Ellen Rawlings. You may remember her as Ellen Bland. Yesterday Mrs. Davison invited us to a cocktail party here. Last night, after Peter Davison took her home, she came to the hotel and waited for us to come in and then told a story about being frightened. Frankly, I didn't take her seriously enough. She seemed pretty mixed up. I wanted to bring her home, but she said that Peter Davison had a cab waiting and would fetch her. Apparently he knew nothing about it."

"That's *his* story."

"Yes. But she got home safely, in some way or other, and told Anne Collier she had talked with us. She apparently retired. A short time later Anne heard the front door close and got up to investigate and Brenda was gone. Anne thought she had left hurriedly because she had taken her evening bag even though she'd dressed in a rough tweed suit."

"A good deal of her jewelry seems to be missing."

Patrick said, "She was wearing a bushel when we saw her at the hotel. She had a small plaster covering a small burn on one wrist which was practically concealed by her bracelets. If all the diamonds and sapphires were real there must have been a fortune in her rings and bracelets."

"Damn fool," grunted Dorn. "That sticking plaster was one way we identified her, by the way. That and her hair and her fingernail polish. This Paula Eastwood was her hair-dresser, you see. Manicurist, too. The Eastwood woman had special bottles of nail enamel for her customers, with their names on the bottles. There's a lot of people to question in this case—all that Eastwood woman's customers, hotel clerks, trainmen, night-club servants. My God! If it hadn't been for a glove which was dropped and overlooked—and if the glove hadn't actually had her name in it—well, that was a break."

"Who is Paula Eastwood?"

"Osterholz," Dorn said. I did not look at Patrick. "She translated her name into English, with the permission of the court, as many Germans did during the war. That part's all in order. She's had a good record according to the F.B.I. The people in the house where she has an apartment all say that she was quiet and well-behaved."

"What did she look like?"

"Typical blonde German woman. Thirty-one years old. She worked in a number of Fifth Avenue beauty shops before she started up her own business."

Patrick said, "There was a man named von Osterholz at Brenda Davison's party yesterday afternoon." Dorn opened his eyes a little rounder. "He had a sort of fit. Heart attack, apparently." Dorn's stenographer made a note of it. "I'd like to meet the guy again myself," Patrick said. "Last night an attack was made on my wife and me in Central Park. Later on, a tall man in a gray suit followed us into our hotel room, pushed my wife down on her face and knocked me down, then ran. If you want the real lowdown, that's why I'm on this case. I want to get even with that guy."

"Did you report all that to the police?"

"There was nothing conclusive to report."

"You are sure the man who attacked you was von Osterholz?"

"I'm not at all sure. I think it's likely."

"You think he wanted to kill you?"

"Nope. I think he merely wanted me out of the way. Wanted us to leave town, maybe. Made himself a sort of super-nuisance."

Dorn shook his head, a slight shake. He didn't see it, apparently, in that light.

"You said he had a heart attack?"

"His heart was going lickety-split. Could have been too much benzedrine, maybe."

"And afterwards you saw him in the Park?"

"I didn't see his face. The light wasn't good enough."

Patrick described the incident. "A taxicab came to our rescue. Osterholz—if he was it—and another who acted as his chauffeur beat it."

"Do you know the name of that cab driver?"

I held my breath. That would mean turning in Tony Konrad.

"Yes," Patrick said.

"It might be useful. Then, later, this same man trailed you to your room?"

"I don't know that it was the same man. Could have been, though. A tall man in a gray suit, with red hair, was seen running out of our corridor just at that time. The incident roused the suspicion of a woman he passed in the hall. She called the house detectives. One named Evans came up to check up."

Dorn looked owlish. "You told him it might have been this von Osterholz?"

"Nope. I told him nothing. We couldn't've identified the man had they rounded him up."

"And, of course, it didn't occur to either of you that Peter Davison is a tall lean fellow with red hair. And that he probably owns a gray suit. In fact, he's wearing one this morning."

"That's just silly," I said. "Pete wouldn't do a thing like that. He wouldn't run in behind us and knock us down."

"He wouldn't get on a train and ride in one direction an hour or two and then get off and ride right back again either, I suppose?"

"That's different. Besides, why would he want to hurt us?"

"He'd spent the evening with Brenda Davison. If she told Anne Collier she was getting herself a private detective why wouldn't she tell young Davison the same thing? She seems to have been rather gone on Davison, by the way, so it's more than likely she did."

Patrick sat forward a trifle.

"Who reported the murder, Lieutenant?"

"The superintendent at the apartment house. He lived on the floor below the Eastwood woman. Seems he heard people walking about and thought maybe she was sick, so he went up to inquire. Something suspicious had occurred a few minutes before he went up. He'd opened the front door for what he took to be the milkman, but he hadn't heard the man come in and go upstairs."

We sat listening.

"The superintendent gets up very early. They have to. One of the things he always does is to let the milkman into the main hall. That is, the milkman rings his bell and he pushes the buzzer which releases the lock on the door between the entrance hall and the main hall. This morning after opening the door he didn't hear the usual sound of bottles and such. Then he heard stealthy footsteps overhead. So he reconnoitered. After ringing the Eastwood bell and getting no results he got suspicious. So he pounded on the door. That fetched his wife upstairs. Too bad—if she had stayed in their apartment she would have seen the murderers leaving the place."

"Murderers?" I cried.

He took it that the plural was what surprised me.

"There was a man and a woman. The man was tall and slim, like Peter Davison. The woman was medium tall and wore a very fancy hat." He looked at mine as if it was the first time he had noticed it. "Something like yours, Mrs. Abbott. The milkman actually saw the pair—they had the colossal nerve to let him in when he arrived and rang, and the superintendent and his wife were both upstairs, having meantime discovered the body. The superintendent had let himself into the Eastwood apartment with his passkey—you see—when no one came to the door."

"The milkman could identify the pair?" Patrick asked.

"He said he would know the woman. He looked at her instead of the man, on account of the hat."

"Imagine a milkman noticing hats," I said.

Dorn let it pass. "The Eastwood dame went in for fancy clothes, so there's not much doubt who the woman was, and it's dollars to doughnuts the man was Peter Davison."

Patrick said, "How many doughnuts, Lieutenant?"

"What?"

"That the pair were not Pete Davison and Paula Eastwood?"

Dorn said, "You're wasting time. At least we're fairly sure it was the Eastwood woman. The man . . ."

Patrick said, "The man was me, Lieutenant."

Dorn stiffened. His stenographer seized his pencil. I sat still, watching the policeman, wondering if he would believe us, terrified that he would not, and just as terrified that he would.

"Now, see here, Abbott! No funny business, please. We're short of men, and what with all the people we've got to talk to in this case . . ."

"Well, at least I can save you chasing up this one red herring, Dorn. The man was me and the woman was my wife. Look at her hat."

The round blue eyes fixed themselves on my flossy hat.

"I don't get it, Abbott."

"Let me talk, Dorn. We were tailed in the Park and then followed into our hotel room. In the Park the man had a gun. He leveled it on us but he wasn't quite certain of his aim, or maybe he just hestitated. He never fired the gun. When he got close enough we had a tussle over it, and when the taxicab showed up he managed to snatch the gun away and ran. In the hotel he pushed my wife down on the floor in order to get at me, but he only gave me a slight crack on the head, and then again he ran. Why? Probably because his nerve failed him. The hotel is efficiently patrolled. When he got right down to it maybe he lacked the courage to finish the job." The lieutenant squirmed, but assumed an air of patience as Patrick said, "Not long after the man followed us to our room for what you might call the abortive attack, the Davison agent, Harold Couch, phoned that Brenda Davison was missing from her apartment. He called me because Anne Collier told him that Brenda had engaged my services, which she hadn't, definitely, but maybe she thought she had. We came over here and met Couch and the Ashbrooks and decided to do nothing until daylight because we didn't want to embarrass Brenda if she showed up shortly and had gone out of her own accord."

"You mean, they thought she had gone off with Pete Davison?"

"That's what they thought."

"Did you?"

"No. Not specifically."

"Why not?"

I said, "Because Pete wasn't in love with Brenda, Lieutenant Dorn!"

The lieutenant looked at me, and back at Patrick.

"The Ashbrooks and the agent Couch left the apartment before we did. Now, Anne had been waked by the front door closing. But apparently Brenda went down by way of the service elevator. The man on the front elevators was alone on the job, and he was new. He said he didn't know Brenda by sight. But anyone with eyes would notice Brenda Davison."

"Then how did she go out?"

"By the service elevator, as I said. She may have changed her mind after leaving her apartment by the front door, and walked back and took herself down."

"Why?"

"To avoid being seen."

"You think she went out alone?"

"No, I don't. But I think it's possible. She had a private phone. She might have made a date and slipped out alone. I incline to the idea, however, that she was forced in some way to leave the house. I agree with my wife that had she been keeping a rendezvous she wouldn't have been so careless as to carry an evening bag with a tweed suit."

"All her jewels are gone," Dorn said.

"I didn't know that last night. By the way, she may have gone away on the river. I've got this."

Patrick brought out the glove Tony Konrad had said he had found on the boat landing.

Dorn examined it.

"It looks like the mate to the one in the Eastwood apartment."

"It certainly does."

"You found it?"

"No. Our cab driver found it. He was poking around while we were up-stairs. This same man had told me that just after we were attacked in our room a tall man came out and took another cab to 89th and York. He thought the man was the one who had held us up in the Park. He was the cab driver who came to our rescue in the Park, incidentally."

"Remarkable cab driver!" snorted the Law.

"Remarkable in a city famous for remarkable cab drivers."

"What's his name?"

"I'll give it—on one condition," Patrick said. Dorn frowned. "The condi-tion is all in your favor. You're to follow him, if you like, but not to question him unless I agree to it. If he's one of a gang that's what you'd want to do, isn't it, Lieutenant?"

Dorn took a minute. He nodded. Patrick gave Tony Konrad's name and license number.

"Now, in our hotel room, before Couch called saying that Brenda had left so mysteriously, I'd busied myself among other things looking up Osterholzes in the phone book." I recalled how Pat had leafed through the book while I was in my bath. "The book didn't yield much, either with or without the *von*. So I tried the translation—Easterwood and Eastwood. There was this Paula, on 89th Street near York. Paula is a common German name. They rarely translate the Christian name, as you know. Paula was located near 89th and York, also near the East River. Tony had told us about the tall man in the raincoat taking a cab to 89th and York. Tony had found the glove on the boat landing. Playing a wild hunch that Brenda might have been taken away by boat, and that her destination was Paula Eastwood's apartment, I headed up there—well, you know the rest."

"Tony take you up there?"

"No. We came back to the hotel first."

"How did you get into the Eastwood apartment?"

"The superintendent—or caretaker as you sometimes call him—pushed the buzzer. The front door of the Eastwood apartment was open a crack."

"Open? Why?"

"My opinion is that the murderer wanted the body discovered."

"Good God! Why?"

"I can't answer that, yet."

"Why didn't you report the murder to the police?"

"I should have—but the superintendent arrived, and I knew he would do it. Put yourself in my place."

"In your place I should have done my duty."

"Right. But, remember, Dorn, it was a matter of explaining not to the police but to the superintendent and the milkman and a screaming woman how
we happened to be in that apartment. No, thanks. I didn't want to get into
that, just then. I had other fish to fry."

"What?"

"Things to think out. Stuff like that."

Dorn shrugged. "So you walked out the back door and got out through the
caretaker's apartment and opened the door for the milkman."

"Right."

"I'll be damned!"

There was a silence, then Dorn said, "I don't see why a fellow like you
who belongs out on the Coast doesn't stay put."

"But we are here on a vacation!" I said.

"That's what you said the other time."

"It's true. But you know how people are, don't you? A detective is just like
a doctor. If people have problems, they'll get you involved before you know
it."

Dorn said nothing. I said that anyway Patrick was trying to retire, that we
were going to have a ranch. I didn't say anything about yearning for the
patter of small feet, feeling that the stuffy police lieutenant would not appre-
ciate the thought. But I said enough, it seems, for him to yearn for my absence, because, abruptly, he suggested that he would prefer to talk with Patrick
alone.

The worst had come true. I was excluded—kicked out, though politely—
from the room, and therefore I was going to miss something.

Sadly I walked along the hall and upstairs. I walked into Katy's nursery.
The door was open on the terrace. I could hear Katy laughing and I could
hear the humming from the great bridge.

I walked to the door. Pete Davison and Anne Collier faced each other
beside the railing. They were both angry.

Leaning against the wall near the door was a police sergeant with a heart-
shaped shiny-eyed face. He was Sergeant—erstwhile Patrolman—Goldberg.
He was gazing cheerfully at the flowing river far below and I'm sure he
heard nothing equivocal as Anne Collier said, "You're a cute boy, Pete. The
trouble with you is your timing. So thanks, but I've changed my mind."

11

There is a gloss from Europe which hangs forever over New York. It is the least American of our cities. You are always running into Europeans and you keep hearing snatches of European languages. A flock of French restaurants blooms in a narrow midtown street. All over the city, uptown, downtown, midtown, the eating places pop up—Swedish, Italian, German, Russian, Spanish, Hungarian. The alien smells of garlic, chives, paprika and anise float in the air, routing the native salt tang of the sea.

Most of all this gloss shows itself with the people like Elizabeth and Clive Ashbrook, a type not uncommon in New York and so veneered by long residence abroad they no longer seem American at all.

Standing on the terrace outside Katy Davison's living room—the day nursery—I could hear Elizabeth's froggy notes in a conversation with Clive Ashbrook's deep tones and Harold Couch's dry ones. They had come at my very heels into the room I had just crossed to come onto the terrace.

At the railing Anne's sweet voice, clear as a bell, said, "I've told you it won't work, Pete. You'd charm me out of using the old brain. We'd end up murdering each other."

"Don't use that word murder," Pete barked out.

"Hello, kids," I called. "How are you, Sergeant Goldberg?"

The sergeant, having two years ago convinced himself that my wedding ring was the real McCoy, met me with shiny glances and a frank friendly handshake. Anne came hurrying, Pete strolled to meet me, not very happy because I had broken in at a time when he'd rather I hadn't. Katy treadled over, got off her trike and offered her small gloved hand with her prim little dip.

"Where is Pat?" Anne asked. "There's something I've got to tell him. I should have last night, but then it would have been spilling a confidence. Now . . . Now . . ."

Her lips trembled. Pete Davison came up and put an arm around her. Anne allowed it, for the moment, to remain.

Sergeant Goldberg coughed discreetly. The cough said, "Don't you kids do or say anything compromising, see? On account of because I've got to report it to the lieutenant." Anne slipped out of the encircling arm and Pete jammed his hands into his pockets.

"Pat's with Lieutenant Dorn," I said.

"Do you think he'll be allowed to talk to me alone?" Anne asked.

"I think so, pretty soon."

From the day nursery Elizabeth Ashbrook's voice drifted out, insidious and toneful. "She said that the American male says nix on hips—buttocks, *au contraire*." The men chuckled and Elizabeth said, "My God! She didn't show an inch of flesh or make one vulgar motion but she puts plenty across the footlights. She's tremendously vulgar but she's funny. Her audiences laugh without the least self-consciousness. She does you good." She came out on the terrace and, seeing us, said, "I'm raving about an English music-hall actress who's about to descend on New York. Hello, Jean." She gave me her long firm hand. "You don't mind if I call you Jean?" She turned from me to Katy, stooping down, her rugged features taking on a special tenderness. Certainly no madonna to look at, Elizabeth's green eyes were rich with pure mother love as her attention to the child seemed to exclude everything else.

I shook hands with Clive Ashbrook. His suave fingers managed a faint but knowing pressure. I was so astonished I couldn't meet his glance. I felt my color coming up, making itself a nuisance. I freed my hand and gave it to Mr. Couch. He was grave and tired-looking. The family had been together before Pat and I had arrived. The Ashbrooks and the agent were now just up from breakfast, served them by Brenda's servants, who had come in at seven o'clock.

Elizabeth Ashbrook was dressed in the same or a similar navy wool dress, under the mink coat, which was draped like a cape around her shoulders. She had on the smart low-heeled shoes which you see so often in New York. She wore no hat. Her red hair, carelessly pulled up on top of her head, looked badly touched up.

Pete Davison said, "Dorn tells me you and Hal identified the body, Clive."

The faces sobered. Ashbrook shuddered and said not to remind him of it. Mr. Couch's mouth tightened.

"It was a pretty nasty task," he said.

"Rather," Pete said. "I've seen the dead in battle. A lot of them chewed up. I should think this might have been pretty much like that."

"It was frightful," Clive said. I caught a gleam in his wife's eye. She was fitting a cigarette into the long black holder. Automatically Clive's hand brought out his lighter, and he was giving her the light as he said—and her eyes met his briefly—"There wasn't much to go on. Her hair. The patch over the burn on her left wrist. That fingernail polish."

Elizabeth said, "Clive is embarrassed. You'd think he'd never seen a naked woman in his life."

"Liz!" Mr. Couch said, flicking a glance at Sergeant Goldberg. The patrolman's glance was still far-flung, apparently focused on the bridge.

Elizabeth made a low mirthful noise in her throat.

"Paula Eastwood is very clever," she said. "A little brown in the lipstick and the same in nail polish, and madame has chic. That cinnamon touch is just what madame the beautiful blonde requires. Madame's coloring is like a valley in the Tyrol in the autumn. This touch of cinnamon brown is the color of the beeches around the golden-green lakes which are so like madame's eyes. Madame will pay for it through the nose, of course. Paula is full of such tricks. That's one reason I stopped going there."

"You know her?" I asked.

The magnificent almond-green eyes rested on me.

"I knew her in Vienna, before she came to New York. I helped her get established here. And she promptly forgot it when she had built up a handsome private clientele and I could no longer afford her."

"She is a Viennese?"

"She's Prussian. Her shop was a branch of her husband's business in Berlin. Vienna was a step on her ladder. Her goal was New York, and she knew that the Viennese have a special piquancy to New Yorkers—impossible in a Berliner. Also, it was easier to get here then from Vienna. The Americans have such sympathy for the Austrian refugees, as she then pretended to be. Special agencies and persons acted as their sponsors. I wonder how Paula got to Vienna? At a time when German nationals weren't allowed to leave their own country? By the way, Sergeant Goldberg, you might ask that lieutenant to analyze the hair."

"Hair?" said Sergeant Goldberg.

"My sister-in-law's hair. I've a notion it was touched up."

"Liz!" Anne cried. She was shocked. She had lured Katy to the other end of the terrace.

"But why not, darling? What difference? Paula is wonderful with hair. Mine has looked like spinach ever since I gave her up."

"Why did you give her up?" I asked.

"Money, my dear. Didn't I say that? For three years Paula and such extravagances have been out of my world."

"Well," Pete said. "Don't cry about it, Liz. You can go back to her now."

"How amusing you are, Pete!"

"Please!" said Mr. Couch.

Elizabeth said to her brother, "Believe it or not, I never wanted things enough to get them this way, Pete. As a matter of fact I never really regretted giving up such items as Paula Eastwood. She is a swine. That place of hers is amusing, though. Like a private bordello, all red plush and rayon brocade and French dolls and stuff."

Clive said, in his rich voice, "You always did say she was a calculating creature, Liz."

"So I did. But, honestly, I never even imagined her homicidal. I can only suspect that seeing Brenda loaded down with diamonds and sapphires she lost her head. Maybe she longed for Germany again. They all do. Maybe she thought she could make a haul and sell the stuff and retire."

"Why would Brenda go there at that hour of the night?" I asked.

There was a grain of malice in Elizabeth's eyes as she said, "Paula sometimes lets her place for—dates. She is very accommodating if there's money. I dare say that sin, in such a setting, would seem the genuine article."

Clive Ashbrook smiled. Sergeant Goldberg blushed.

"Liz, I beg you to be careful!" Mr. Couch said. "People don't always understand your jokes, dear."

Elizabeth said, "Hal, why should we be hypocrites? We never liked Brenda, and you know it. The important thing is now to be frank and tell what we know and help the police find out who killed her. There *will* be a scandal. We can't stop that now. I don't know that I care much. But I'd like to see Paula Eastwood and her accomplice—if she has any—drawn and quartered. If the result is a public exhibition of the Davison heirs—so what?"

I asked, "Was her name Osterholz in Vienna?"

Elizabeth's eyes veiled. "At that time she called herself Frau Wagner."

"I don't believe what you—what you inferred," Anne said, coming over. "I think Brenda was perfectly sweet and good. I don't think she ever did anything really wrong. You always try to be so sophisticated, Liz. Brenda wasn't. I think you may be right, though, in thinking that she was killed for her rings and bracelets. But I think the murderer came for her here. I think she was forced to leave this house taking her loot with her, and then taken up there against her will and murdered. Why would she have been wearing her jewelry? She'd undressed. She'd taken off her evening clothes. So she must have removed her rings and things. She didn't wear all that jewelry to bed."

"Maybe you're right about Brenda's character, Anne," Elizabeth said, indifferent now.

"Let's hope you are, Anne," Mr. Couch said.

Pete Davison said nothing. He was very taciturn this morning, and he was watchful.

Elizabeth turned to me. "I want to talk to your husband, Jean. I can give him the lowdown on Paula, at least."

Clive Ashbrook said, "I hope her jewelry was properly insured, Hal."

"Yes, I think it was," Mr. Couch said. "I just recently sent along her policies to be renewed."

"Oh, for God's sake," Pete exploded.

Clive said, "But the insurance companies have the best detectives, Pete. They'll trace the jewels. That's the quickest way to catch the murderers."

"As Clive said, the insurance people do have excellent detectives," Mr.

Couch said. "If anybody can catch a thief, they can. The Eastwood woman at least should be fairly easy to find."

"Greedy blonde bitch," said Elizabeth.

A young policeman came to the door and told Mr. Couch that he was to come at once to Lieutenant Dorn. Five minutes later Patrick showed up. Elizabeth nailed him at once for a private interview. I felt disappointed when he put her off till afternoon. So was she. He had a lot of leg work to do first, he said. Without taking a chance on being left behind, I walked over and stood beside him. As we waited outside the apartment for the elevator to come up Patrick said that he had met Mr. Couch on his way upstairs and had dated him for lunch. He said also that the police couldn't find the new elevator man who was on duty here last night. He had given a phony home address, and forged references. He was therefore probably a link in the chain of the planned abduction and murder of Brenda Davison.

"If that is what it is," he added, cynically.

12

The middle-aged woman with a face like a silvery cat sat in the blue chair and her blue eyes went again to the sweet little Dresden clock on the white-painted mantel-piece. Her hands fidgeted. She wore a rosy-pink nail enamel and her rouge and lipstick matched.

"As I told you, I know nothing about my late husband's business affairs," she said.

"He never spoke to you about his patients?"

"Naturally, but hardly ever by name. That would be a violation of a doctor's ethics, you see."

That wasn't entirely the reason, lady, I was thinking, as Patrick questioned the relict of the late Dr. Amos Crossland. She was probably as giddy as the clock on the mantelpiece, which was running gaily along half an hour fast.

"Will you permit me to look at his case records, Mrs. Crossland?"

"Oh, I don't know. Oh, no. I couldn't, even if I had them. We sold his practice, you see."

"When?"

The pretty old face smiled as in a sad dream. "I don't know the exact date. My lawyers took care of all that. My poor husband! I shouldn't want you to think he deliberately killed himself. I still can't believe it. He was so quiet and easy-going, right up till the end. When they told me it was suicide I said they were insane." She glanced at the clock. "I have a luncheon, you see."

"Your clock is fast," Patrick said. She accepted his statement without either believing or questioning him. She made no move to do anything about the dilly of a Dresden clock. She herself was a dilly. She was not over five feet tall. She wore a pink quilted robe and looked like a doll.

Now why would a doctor marry anybody like that, I wondered. Don't be silly, I then said to myself. She can get married any day, even yet. She is as pretty as a picture right now and she's obviously crowding sixty. She must have been a darling as a girl. He adored her probably. Doctors are like anybody else.

"I suppose," she said, "that you are who you say you are, Mr. Abbott, because you have showed me those papers from the police which say I am to give you any information you ask for. But, frankly, I do not like to have my poor husband's suicide dragged up. It still hurts me so terribly, you see. It was only a short time ago, hardly three months, and the shock almost killed me." She believed what she was saying, and that made it so. "You see, my husband was elderly. He was almost sixty-five. But there was the war, and no place really to go for a rest, and besides doctors were so terribly needed. So he stayed on with his practice and he worked himself to death. Suicide while temporarily out of his mind, they said. Overwork. Fatigue." The little clock chimed the hour and its timbre was similar to the pretty woman's voice. "He lay downstairs in his office all night, after he did it—till his nurse arrived in the morning. She found him. The revolver was in his hand. One shot had—had done it. There was no doubt about it. Only his own fingerprints were on the gun. His own gun. I really must ask you to go. I'm lunching with my club, at the Pierre, and I haven't even started to get ready."

"It is exactly twenty-seven minutes to eleven," Patrick said. "Your clock is fast, Mrs. Crossland."

Mrs. Crossland looked at the clock. She said nothing.

"In any case, we won't keep you," Patrick said. I had risen already, so frantic was she to get rid of us, and she was rising, looking very tiny in her delicious silk wrappings. "You say that Dr. Wayland Campbell bought your husband's practice? Where can I find him?" Mrs. Crossland gave an address, just around the corner on Park Avenue. "And the nurse? Your husband's office nurse, wasn't she? How can I get in touch with her?"

"Oh, I've no idea!" the little woman said, with unexpected vigor. "Her association with my husband was pure business, of course. She didn't leave me a forwarding address."

"Perhaps she went to Dr. Campbell?"

"I think not."

"She'd been a long time in your late husband's employ?"

"Oh, yes. Now, if you will excuse me . . ."

"What is her name and the last address you have?"

Impatiently Mrs. Crossland went to her desk. In a very short moment she said, "Her name is Vivian Black. She used to live at 45 East 55th Street." She rang then for her maid to show us out.

Waiting for the elevator to come up I said, "Mrs. C. is jealous of that nurse."

"It looked that way."

"You're checking up on the Davisons, aren't you? You haven't said. You want to know what ailed Katy when she was ill in the winter?"

"Maybe."

"Don't be pixyish, darling. After all, I'm along."

"You're along because I'd rather not have you pushed headlong off one of the terraces of that penthouse, Jeanie. You know too much."

"What do I really know?"

"As much as I do, which is plenty. And you were with me when we found the murdered woman. One of them killed that woman. Believe me, I'm going to pin the crime on the right one."

"Even if it's Pete?"

"Even if it's Pete."

"It couldn't be, Pat."

"Don't let your romantic notions upset your judgment."

In the elevator we were silent, but outside in the fresh clear air which Patrick said was a match for that of Paris at its best, I said, "It wasn't Pete."

"You can't bear to have it Pete. Because he's in love with Anne Collier. Young love must take its true course."

"It's more than that. He wouldn't. If he did, he wouldn't beat her up the way he did afterwards. That's maniacal."

"Maniacal? It was the most deliberate thing the killer did. And he did it calmly. He put a towel over her face so the blood wouldn't splatter and show on his clothes. He did it deliberately to destroy her identity."

"Well, I hope that stuffy Dorn doesn't gang up on Pete."

"Dorn isn't as stuffy as he looks. He's already spotted the love angle. He thinks that Pete murdered Brenda in order to raise some quick cash. He thinks Pete came East to raise money by marrying Brenda if necessary and went off the beam because he fell in love with Anne. He's got evidence which makes Pete look like a very untrustworthy character. The department in this town is on its toes, too. They've checked up pretty thoroughly on what Pete did last night. He didn't tell us the whole truth."

"Darling?"

"Pete did take the cab from the Waldorf to Grand Central. He checked his bag there. But he left the bag in the checkroom. Why? They've got the baggage check. The time he checked the bag in and out was stamped on it. They finger-printed it. His prints are on it."

"That must have been a chore, all the baggage checks which must have accumulated . . ."

"They are equipped to do things like that."

"Probably Pete had a good reason for lying, Pat."

Patrick said grimly, "That's what the police say."

In spite of the credentials Lieutenant Dorn had given Patrick, Dr. Campbell kept us waiting.

"What do you want to know about Dr. Crossland's suicide?" he demanded. He was slender, dark, annoyed and not much interested. "I thought that was settled long ago? There was an autopsy."

"Do you think it possible that Dr. Crossland was murdered, Dr. Campbell?"

"Murdered? Why, in God's name?"

"A doctor must make a few enemies."

"A doctor's worst enemies are the mental cases walking around free as the air when they ought to be shut up."

"Or people the doctor catches trying to do murder."

Dr. Campbell shrugged. "It's hard to imagine even a nut having it in for Crossland. He was a very kind man."

"I've gathered that, Dr. Campbell. But I've a hunch that Crossland was murdered because he knew too much about Katy Davison's illness. Three months ago."

The muscles tightened around the hard jawbones of Dr. Campbell, and the color of his dark eyes seemed darker. "I'm afraid I can't help you in any way, Mr. Abbott. Dr. Crossland left no case records. In that particular instance, I mean."

Patrick tried not to show his excitement. He sat listening as the doctor, having got started, talked on.

"They were not in his files when I took them over. His wife knew nothing about them. I was keenly interested because the Davisons became my patients, and since they are people who frequently call a physician it seemed curious to me that Crossland had no record of any kind on them in his files. As is frequent in medical practice the patients themselves don't know too much about themselves. By that I mean Brenda Davison. The child is of course too young. I have not told them that there are no records. I merely started from scratch with new ones." The doctor put his hands together, clean shining hands, and his lips closed tight as he decided to say nothing more.

Patrick said, "You know that Brenda Davison was found murdered, don't you, Dr. Campbell?"

The doctor's face froze with horror. "My God! When? Where?"

"Early this morning. In a place on East 89th Street. I wonder if you also know that her death will mean that either Pete Davison or Elizabeth Ashbrook will gain custody of the child—who, by the way, has quite a lot of money."

The doctor said, after a moment, "Please don't quote me, but Mrs. Ashbrook is in no physical condition to take on such a job."

"Her heart, I believe."

The doctor's white eyelids covered his black eyes for a fraction of a second. He said, "She is a sick woman. And a very gallant one indeed."

"Her husband looks healthy," Patrick said.

"Ashbrook is sound as a drum."

"Children like Katy are not raised by their parents," Patrick said. (This was not the wild west. He should have said reared.) "With competent nurses and governesses Ashbrook could carry on the job so long as Mrs. Ashbrook lives, couldn't he? His wife will live, I suppose?"

Dr. Campbell said stiffly, "I am not able to predict the life span of my patients, Mr. Abbott. Some of them live much longer than I anticipate, even with deadly diseases. Others in apparently perfect health snap out every day. By the way, your theory that my late colleague Dr. Crossland was murdered interests me. But it doesn't make good sense. I think he just decided to check out and did it. He carried a good deal of insurance. His wife needs money, uses it like water. She is now well provided for. There was no suicide clause in any of his policies. He was worn out. He shot himself. There you are."

"You knew him personally?"

"Very well."

"How well did you know Brenda Davison?"

The doctor again took his time.

"Not very well. Her death is shocking, of course. But she had never consulted me for herself, aside from a check-up I gave her last month. Several times I've been called to the house. She had some notion that the little girl is in danger every minute she is out of that place they live in. I could almost say she is jittery whenever Katy was out of her sight. She was having the fence put around the terrace and special new locks and this and that the first time I was called there after Crossland's death. It struck me as unnecessary and— and unpleasant. Why doesn't she give that place up if she is frightened because of the child? I beg your pardon—what I am saying is now beside the point."

He looked at his watch. Patrick said, "I understand the little girl has a sort of allergy . . ."

The doctor bristled.

"Allergy? It is nothing of the kind! It's a condition. A rare one, we think. This Davison case is the only one I've met where mother and daughter have the same thing! I have a notion that that was why Crossland's records were not in the files. I suspect the doctor took them up to his apartment intending to write the case up for the American Medical Association, and that Mrs. Crossland threw them out. Not intentionally, but she is overly tidy, and she isn't very——businesslike."

"I should like to know the name of the disease, Dr. Campbell."

"Disease? It is not a disease. It is a condition."

"Like haemophilia perhaps?"

"Good God, no. It's nothing at all except that she must never take—well, a certain commonly used drug. It destroys—well, it would kill her. It almost did, in the winter."

"If I knew the name . . ."

"Mr. Abbott," the doctor said gently, "that little girl is very rich, and there might be people, now, or later, who wished—well, I don't want to sound morbid, but people do kill for money. I think her mother guarded the child a bit overzealously, but she had recently had a bad scare. I refer to the child's illness. I can understand her wishing to keep its nature a secret. Rather, I can understand why she thought she must."

"You refer to her somewhat hysterical manner?"

The doctor said, "Frankly, I've been advising Mrs. Davison to consult a psychiatrist."

"Had she done so?"

"I think not."

"Why did you suggest that?"

"Well, things had rather stacked up against her. She had married out of her own way of life. Her husband had met a violent death. She's off the beam. Those things come straight, but it takes time, a long time perhaps."

"And she was shocked when the child was poisoned. . . ."

"Poisoned? It is not the same thing."

"An autopsy—if . . ."

"Would show nothing except that the white corpuscles were reduced below normal. . . . Mr. Abbott! Please! If there was anything to gain in revealing the facts, but there isn't. You might pass the information along. I would merely expose the child to danger if she happens to stand in the way of a ruthlessly ambitious person. That's what worried her mother." He asked, "How did she die?"

"She was slugged in the back of the head and after she was dead her face was pounded to a pulp to prevent her being identified. One of her gloves was, however, found near the body."

"My God! And she wouldn't take common ordinary cold medicines, or a sleeping tablet, for fear of death! She wouldn't even have a trained nurse with Katy. I doubt if she even trusted me. And then this!"

"What about the Davisons? How much do they know about this—ah—condition?"

"Nothing, according to Brenda Davison."

I said, "Clive Ashbrook looks ruthless and ambitious."

"Maybe he does," Dr. Campbell said. "But I doubt if he'd lift a finger to get anything for himself. He doesn't have to. His ability to marry rich women who look after him like a baby is—ah, rather remarkable."

"Elizabeth hasn't much now, has she?" I asked.

"I don't really know," the doctor said, irritated. "Very fascinating case, Mr. Abbott. Leads to interesting speculation on how the condition occurs. Mother and daughter. Is it hereditary, or merely chance? We don't know much about this thing yet. First reported only a few years ago. See here, I'm talking too much."

Patrick got up. "Thanks, Dr. Campbell."

"Don't mention it. I haven't told you anything, Mr. Abbott. Ethics, you know."

Outside, I said, "He told you a few things, didn't he?"

"Enough that I can finish, I hope," Patrick said. "A lot more than I expected. Crossland was murdered. The case records were stolen and no doubt destroyed. We're getting hot, Baby."

In a stationer's on Madison Avenue Patrick bought a map of New York and environs and then made a telephone call. I waited outside, and edged along into a hat shop next door. It was a heavenly day, the windows gleamed, the sky sparkled. It was one of those bandboxes of shops you see all along Madison. There was a black hat on a peg, a skull-cap of flowers. I went in and asked the price. I tried it on. I didn't take it. It didn't become me half so much as my elaborate John-Frederics. Then, suddenly frantic that Patrick might have escaped me, I rushed out and there he was, coming out of the stationery store.

We snagged a taxi. Patrick was in a good humor.

"Everything's fine now, darling."

"Who did you phone, Pat?"

"I tried to get a man I know at Medical Center. He was out. Then I called Dr. Crossland's former nurse. She was out, too, but she's got a roommate, who said she'd be in after two o'clock. I said we'd be there at three."

"You've certainly made up your mind that Crossland was murdered."

"Crossland was murdered."

The taxicab dropped us in front of the lions at the Public Library. There Patrick looked Felix von Osterholz up in a book on continental nobility. He was there all right, along with pages of his ancestors and contemporaries. The name, Patrick said, was an old and honorable one in Germany. Count Felix had been born on March 1, 1904, which would make him now forty-two. He was one of three brothers. In files of old magazines Patrick then dug up some gossip about Elizabeth Davison Emmerman Ashbrook while she lived abroad. There was even a picture of her and the black-browed Count Felix von Osterholz taken on the Venetian Lido in August, 1936. If the picture was a good one he had certainly changed. The caption said that the Count was often seen lately in the society of the fascinating red-headed American, Liz Emmerman.

Cursing because he must hurry so fast, Patrick rushed us downstairs to the newspaper files, where he dug up worlds of material, but we only had time to go over a little of it. One item was an account of Elizabeth Davison's marriage to James Pratt Emmerman at St. Thomas' Church in June, 1921. The striking beauty of the bride and the high social position and great wealth of the groom made the affair an event of the season. There was a detailed description of the wedding party and the bride's trousseau. The wedding gifts were listed. The bride's gift from her father was a strand of 389 matched pearls of the highest quality which had cost at least half a million dollars.

From 1931 to 1937 Liz Emmerman was listed each year as one of the world's ten best-dressed women, according to Paris.

Another item which stayed in my memory was a malicious piece in a scandal sheet dated December 22, 1938.

NO PEARLS

Among many others married today at the City Hall were Elizabeth Emmerman and Clive Tavistock Ashbrook. It was a second marriage for the bride, and the fourth for the groom, his other three ending in divorce. James Pratt Emmerman, first husband of the bride, died from a plunge from a balcony of their Park Avenue apartment in 1931.

Some with long memories may recall that the Davison-Emmerman wedding was an outstanding social event of June, 1921. The bride's present at that time from her father, the potash tycoon Peter John Davison, was a million-dollar pearl necklace. When asked by this reporter if pearls were again in order, the aging millionaire said he was too old and wise now to cast pearls before you-know-what, all of which means nothing because the Ashbrook blood as everybody knows is so blue it's almost purple.

13

Mr. Couch was not in the restaurant when we arrived. The captain showed us to a table previously reserved, and said that Mr. Couch had said to have a drink if we got there first. The waiter went away to fetch our cocktails. Patrick jotted down some notes and I sat looking at the people.

The restaurant was the Longchamps on Madison near 49th. Mr. Couch lunched here nearly every day. His office was just around the corner on 48th, between Madison and Fifth Avenue. When he came in, within ten minutes after ourselves, he ordered himself a dry Manhattan and—after consulting us, and the waiter—the duckling, new green peas and parsley potatoes. We finished with ice cream, and were drinking black coffee before Mr. Couch got down to business. As Brenda's proxy pro tem—the will even specified who should act in the emergency of death of any of the Davison heirs—he must discuss Patrick's fee.

"Anything you say will be all right, Mr. Abbott. My only regret is that we didn't get down to brass tacks last night when we first knew that Brenda was missing."

"Well, how much do you say, Mr. Couch?"

The agent spread out his well-cared-for hands.

"We've had very little experience with these things."

"We?"

"I entered my father's business. He was active in it until only a few years ago, and I still run out to his place in Westchester every few days to consult him. He drew up the Davison will."

"He is a lawyer?"

"Oh, yes. So am I. I don't do any court work, but my father did a little right up until his retirement a few years ago. By the way, if you meet him, don't use that word retirement. He's eighty-six and he hasn't been active in the office for several years, but he still takes a hearty interest in all the business—in fact, I always consult him when anything bothers me. I hate to tell him about this murder thing. It will be a personal shock. Old Mr. Davison was a friend of my father's."

"Your father drew up his will, you said."

"Yes. If anybody can make a will that's unbreakable it's my old father. They used to call him *the* will-lawyer."

"To an outsider, Mr. Couch, the Davison will seems grossly unfair."

"Yes," Mr. Couch said, "and no. To men like Mr. Davison and my father, both self-made—tough old hardheads, both of them—anything looked better than to leave good money to people who would throw it away. Elizabeth has spent a fortune. Jack—Brenda's husband—spent money like water on his various schemes. Pete had a good business head, but he wouldn't come home and go into his father's business. So old Davison decided to take a chance on the grandchild not yet born." Mr. Couch paused. "The old man couldn't stand Clive Ashbrook. That's no secret. Jim Emmerman—Liz's first husband—had got away with a lot of Davison money. When Elizabeth married Ashbrook, who had never turned what Mr. Davison called an honest penny in his life, the old man couldn't take it. But he was fond of his daughter. He waited a good while before he drew up that will."

I said, "You mean, Clive Ashbrook is dishonest?"

Mr. Couch's blue eyes rested on me and then, looking back at Patrick he said, "I'm afraid I'm being pretty frank."

"That's all right, Mr. Couch. My wife is entirely in my confidence."

Inside I glowed. Now that was big of Pat, considering that I was here right this minute just because he felt I was safer when in his sight.

The agent's smile was nice. "You young people are remarkable. But I married a competent woman myself. She died ten years ago, and I sort of muddle around in the same apartment, wondering why I don't move to a hotel. But I've got a good man to do for me, and it's home, even without her." My heart went out to him, but he didn't ask for sympathy, and being businesslike, he got straight back to the Davisons'. "I want to correct any impression I may have given that Clive Ashbrook is dishonest. On the contrary. He's a fine chap. He simply wasn't brought up to work. He was an only child of a very charming woman. She lived abroad. Clive went to school in Switzerland and in England. They hadn't a lot of money, but Clive married young the first time. That wife was a very rich woman. She was also a thoroughly selfish one."

"So Ashbrook was married before?" Patrick asked, as if he didn't know.

"Three times before. Divorced three times."

I said, "My goodness!"

"That doesn't look so good for Ashbrook," Patrick said.

"In their world that sort of thing happens," Mr. Couch said. "And I must say, there is no real malice or rancor in the man. He is devoted to Elizabeth. Incidentally, he never asked for a penny from any of his wives."

"He sounds a bit dumb," Patrick said.

"He isn't, Mr. Abbott. He's simply not money-minded, in any way."

"What would happen if he were stranded without a rich wife to look after him, Mr. Couch?"

"Literally, he'd starve."

"He wouldn't do murder?"

"Good Lord, no!" Mr. Couch said. He believed it, too. But I myself felt suspicious. Tall, dark, and too handsome. Eyes that behaved, that bent on Elizabeth fond glances, but hands inclined to wander, if the pressure he had given mine there on the terrace was any sign. "The police checked on him first thing. He has a perfect alibi. Brenda must have been killed about the time we were all together there in her apartment. Or a little earlier. We know approximately when she left, because the door in closing woke Anne Collier. Anne phoned me at once. I called you and then the Ashbrooks. Clive himself answered the phone. They live in a hotel which is, of course, carefully patrolled. No one could slip in or out of the St. Regis at that hour and not be seen."

Patrick said, "It wouldn't occur to me that Ashbrook would do the murder himself."

Mr. Couch gave his head a quick shake.

"I'm afraid I've prejudiced you against him. In speaking of his many marriages, I mean. I say, and I'll stand by it, that Clive Ashbrook hasn't any selfishness in him. And, something else—he never ran after any of the women he married. They went after him. Liz will tell you that herself."

The guy sounded pretty pallid to me. The more Mr. Couch praised him the less I trusted him.

"Didn't Elizabeth know her father would cut down her money if she married him, Mr. Couch?"

"Of course she knew, Mrs. Abbott. At least, he warned her. He was fond of her. She was his favorite. She probably thought he wouldn't do it. He did."

"How old is Ashbrook?" Patrick asked.

"In his middle forties. A few years older than Elizabeth."

"I should like to know more about the estate. And the various incomes from it."

"I am not at liberty to give you figures, Mr. Abbott. Except one—Katy's guardian, who has been her mother, gets a fixed sum, $25,000 a year, to be used as the guardian sees fit. Any surplus is to be reinvested for the child. This is tax-free. That is, the estate absorbs the taxes, as well as those on Katy's own income, which is about five times that of her mother, her uncle and her aunt."

Patrick whistled. "Then Brenda had the twenty-five grand, her own income from the estate, and Katy's?"

"She didn't have the free use of Katy's income. Any expenditures had to have our sanction. She's used the whole of the twenty-five thousand allowed her as guardian up till now, but all of Katy's own income has been reinvested."

"The heirs with the smaller incomes have had to pay the taxes on the larger ones?"

"Yes. You must understand that Mr. Davison didn't anticipate the big war taxes, however."

"In that case, why didn't the other heirs appeal?"

"They've planned to. But Pete has not been available. And Brenda has not been very co-operative. Naturally."

Patrick said, "How come old Mr. Davison never got the notion that his daughter-in-law might also have been a fortune-hunter, Mr. Couch? Same as Ashbrook?"

"Well, he did," Mr. Couch waited a moment. "I think I'll tell you something. It is strictly between ourselves, remember. Mr. Davison put detectives on Brenda's trail after she married Jack. She said she was an orphan, and that her people had lived in the country, a big place in northern Illinois. A sort of estate. They never traced her for sure, but thought she might be one of seven children from a Polish-American family in South Dakota. If so, she left home at sixteen, managed to get to Chicago, got a job, managed to take a business course, and by the time she was twenty-one she was Jack's private secretary in a radio business he'd started up with offices in Chicago. She was always a very smart girl. Mr. Davison himself stopped the investigation. He was always sorry he'd started it. He liked a girl who could look after herself."

"Did she ever make any voluntary statement to you about her origin?"

"Yes. But it's not the same story."

"If she's got any people they ought to be informed," Patrick said.

"Yes. They can't do anything about her money, however. It all goes back into the estate. Her personal belongings go to Katy. Including her jewelry, if we get it back."

"By the way, what about the insurance on that stuff?"

"I checked on that this morning. She had let the policies lapse. I don't understand it. There was a lot of it, you know. Brenda put every spare penny into stones. Not the best investment, in my opinion. But that's what she wanted."

"After checking on her Mr. Davison was willing to take a chance on leaving most of his estate to her child? It doesn't quite click, Mr. Couch."

"He liked her. He had worked up from common people himself. He liked it in her. She came from good honest hard-working people, just as he did. He didn't think it strange that she'd cut away from her family because he had done the same thing when he left home. He thought she would be thrifty, too. She was—if you consider jewels a good risk."

"What comprises the Davison estate?"

"Old Mr. Davison sold out everything he owned several years ago and invested the money in gilt-edged securities."

"You have a free hand with those?"

"Good Lord, no, Mr. Abbott. When any comes due the money has to be reinvested in the same or a similar sort of thing. And with the say-so of all the heirs. And that's another thing. Lately we've been buying government bonds, which will yield under three per cent instead of five and six. So even with tax relief in prospect the future Davison incomes aren't going to get any bigger."

"But the twenty-five grand paid Katy's guardian will remain fixed-? Until Katy is twenty-one?"

Mr. Couch nodded. Patrick said, "No wonder that job is coveted. The old man fixed up plenty of trouble for that little girl, Mr. Couch."

"He meant it for the best, Mr. Abbott."

"By the way, he must have spent money himself for jewels in his day? He once bought Elizabeth a very fine pearl necklace."

Mr. Couch nodded. "That is one of the things he always held against her. She sold the pearls and squandered the money. But Liz could have anything she wanted when she was a girl. She was a great beauty, you know. And she was smart. That's a good while ago. Now, about your fee?"

"Oh, yes. I don't want to take a fee for myself, Mr. Couch. We're in this too, you see."

Mr. Couch's high blue-veined forehead creased.

"I'd like to lay hands on the man, or men, or man and woman—whatever it is—that did that murder. Partly because they gave us a couple of bad shake-ups last night." Patrick told him briefly of the affair in the Park and the one later on in the hotel. "One of them calls himself Count Felix von Osterholz."

"You mean, the man that fainted?"

"It was a heart attack, Mr. Couch."

"You mean—I don't understand?"

"The man may have brought the heart attack on himself because he is a coward and had to dose himself with benzedrine to get up nerve enough to come to the party. He probably came to the party to get the lay-out of the apartment, or to get a good look at his prospective victim, Brenda Davison. I think he may have taken an overdose of the stimulant and knocked himself out. In the Park he was certainly cowardly. He ran for it the minute another car showed up. In the hotel he may have noticed a uniformed guard as he followed us up to our room. He certainly wouldn't've gone to all the trouble and risk of following us to the room just to give me a tap on the head. He wanted me out of the way, at least for last night. He didn't know, of course, that my interest in the Davisons amounted to less than nothing until he and his pals started trouble for Jean and myself. So I've got my own score to settle and I don't want to be paid for that."

"But why would he want to kill Brenda?"

"Maybe for her jewels. Now, about that fee. What would you say to making it, instead, a reward?"

"A reward?"

"There's a cab driver named Tony Konrad. Tony saw us being shadowed last night. Tony tipped me off that a man who resembled the man who gave us some trouble in the Park had headed for 89th and York, after following us back to the Waldorf. Tony picked up one of Brenda's gloves on the boat-landing behind the apartment house while I was in her place with you and the Ashbrooks. He gave it to me when we came out, just after you and the Ashbrooks left. Thanks to his tips, we found the body."

"You found the body?"

"I should have told you that to start with, Mr. Couch. I've already reported it to the police. We left the scene of the murder pronto, because we could hardly explain our being in the Eastwood apartment to the superintendent and the milkman."

"Great Scott! Why—why, you're amazing, Mr. Abbott. I don't wonder Brenda wanted your services. Why—why . . ."

"There's nothing amazing about it. The little man was doing my leg work, that's all. He wants to buy a place in the country. He deserves the money, not I."

"You're very generous, Mr. Abbott. I'll have to take it up with Pete and Elizabeth, but I'm sure they'll agree. How much, would you say?"

"How about three thousand?"

"Well—that sounds all right to me."

Patrick looked at his watch. "This has been very pleasant, Mr. Couch. By the way, I've been trying to dig some information out of Dr. Wayland Campbell. Next, I'm seeing Dr. Crossland's former nurse. Did you know Dr. Crossland?"

"Of course. He was our doctor for many years."

"Mr. Couch, do you think Crossland was murdered?"

"Murdered? Crossland? Why?"

"I think he was. I think he was murdered because he knew too much about Katy Davison's illness." Mr. Couch sat with his mouth open, aghast with astonishment and horror. "The case records on both Katy and Brenda were not in his files when Dr. Campbell took over. Dr. Campbell suggested that the records might have been in Crossland's apartment. He says the case is unusual, and that Crossland may have been preparing an article, and that the records might have been thrown out accidentally by Mrs. Crossland. I believe nothing of the sort. I think the doctor was murdered and the records taken and destroyed because he knew an attempt had been made to murder either Brenda or Katy Davison. Perhaps both."

Fifteen minutes later, I said, as we were walking along Madison Avenue, on our way to see Vivian Black, Dr. Crossland's former nurse, "You sort of piled things up on Mr. Couch."

"I didn't know any other way to do it. He's acting for Brenda, so he has to know what we know. And there's no time to deal it out a piece at a time. But there was one thing I didn't tell him, Jean. I don't trust him entirely to keep things to himself. His loyalty to the house of Davison is pretty strong. There's no tie like money, Baby."

"What didn't you tell him, Pat? I thought you didn't leave out a thing."

Patrick looked down at me out of the corners of his eyes.

"I didn't tell him that the murdered woman was not Brenda Davison," he said.

14

I was stunned.

Then, very suspicious.

I asked, "How do you know?"

Patrick said airily, "I know you don't think much of my artistic ability."

"I never said so."

"Of course not. You're my ideal wife. But whenever I mention getting away from it all to paint a few pictures—and why not? Look at Winston Churchill!—well, you immediately think how nice it would be for me to raise prize horses or take a trip. Or this or that. You'd better watch your thinking. I'm a mind reader."

"Darling! But look, you're wrong about Brenda. There's the hair? The glove? The fingernail polish?"

"How long does it take that stuff to dry?"

"Oh, twenty minutes or half an hour. To make it really dry. Why?"

"And how long after that does the smell stick around?"

"I don't know. A long while, if you don't do some ventilating. Why?"

Patrick grinned. "And I thought you had such a super smeller, Jeanie."

"Don't be coy, Pat. What do you mean?"

"The air in that room reeked of the banana oil which that nail stuff always smells of."

"Oh. I remember that now. I thought it was bananas. There were some . . ."

"In the kitchen. Too far away. What you smelled was banana oil. The fingernails of the corpse had recently been painted with the enamel Paula Eastwood mixed specially for Brenda Davison. I checked her special bottle of the stuff in the cabinet in the beauty shop. In true German fashion the methodical Paula had the bottle for each customer carefully labeled. Brenda's had been opened a short time before we arrived. There was a tiny drop, still damp, which had oozed below the screw-on cap. There were no fingerprints on the bottle. If there had been I would have taken it away. The smell in the parlor was specially strong because Paula, like all good upstanding Germans, would dislike night air except in midsummer. If she were really a super-duper German she probably would think night-air unhealthy all the year round."

"Was the enamel on the fingernails still sticky?"

"No. It felt dry to the touch. It was probably the first thing the murderer did after beating up the face. It was planned, of course. The whole crime was hideously deliberate."

"But the glove?"

"Also deliberate. To get the corpse labeled Brenda."

"What about the other glove? The one on the landing?"

"I haven't made up my mind on that."

"What about the hair?"

"I suggested that Dorn have the hair analyzed. He answered somewhat stiffly that that would be routine, since the face of the corpse was destroyed. There'll be a complete autopsy and there are plenty of ways of telling that the body isn't Brenda."

"Elizabeth suggested there on the terrace before you came up that Brenda might have had her hair touched up. She also said that Paula Eastwood was a greedy blonde bitch—Pat, is *it* Paula Eastwood?"

"Maybe."

"You think so, don't you?"

"I do."

"Did you tell Lieutenant Dorn that?"

"I did not. Does a guy walk up to a homicide squad and say he doesn't think a corpse is who it's supposed to be because he's seen naked women in art studios and therefore he knows those curves aren't Brenda's? They'd ask then if he'd seen Brenda naked and he says no and they guffaw and when he says he can tell pretty much what their shape is even though thoroughly covered they put him down as an accessory or a dope. No, thanks. There's some risks I don't take."

"Darling, Lieutenant Dorn never guffawed in his life. I'd like him better if he had a couple of good guffaws in him, in fact. But you're evading. You didn't want to tip them off yet. Why not say so?"

"Oke. I say it now. They'll know quick enough. Maybe they do by now. Then what? They'll think Brenda is an accomplice. If not, how come her glove was in the place? Motive? Jealousy or something."

"What do you yourself think about Brenda?"

"I don't know. Couch's sidelights on the girl were too sketchy. I suspect he glossed her over a bit. I'm sure he knows more than he's telling. He did say she was smart. Maybe she's too smart. Or thinks she is, rather."

"You didn't tell Mr. Couch the corpse wasn't Brenda. You held out on him, too."

"I didn't want him talking. It would be a hard thing to keep silent about, in his position. Maybe I shouldn't've told him about going there and finding the body either. I was afraid the police might spill it and I wanted to tell him before they did. I don't want our clients to think were holding out on them, but, frankly, Couch is the only one I trust with information like that. Even so, I'd rather not tell him yet that it isn't Brenda."

"Darling, I adore Pete."

"Pete's swell. I also have a yen for Liz, just between ourselves, but I wouldn't trust either of them not to talk. Liz, after all, is married to the handsome Clive Ashbrook. And Pete would be much too anxious to do something drastic too pronto."

"I don't like the way you've been holding out on me, but I'll admit I asked for it. I'm slipping. I should have spotted that banana oil smell. It's more sickening than that from fresh bananas. However, I couldn't tell what Brenda looked like stripped. I've never had the advantage of sitting in life classes and eyeing nude models. Not me. When the corpse's waist looked smaller than you'd think and her hips wider I just thought that Brenda had managed that extra-lithe look with a hundred-dollar corset. Besides, I was feeling sick."

"You were swell. A weak woman would have urped."

"Well, thanks for *that* compliment, anyway. Was the nail polish put on evenly, or was it messy?"

Patrick snorted angrily.

"It was even enough. The bastard who did that job is a cold, unfeeling brute."

"Then it wasn't our friend von Osterholz?"

"Why not? He may be cool enough when he's sure he won't get caught in the act."

A car slid up and braked. "Why not ride and take a load off your feet, Bud and Lady?" Tony Konrad asked.

I suppressed a gasp. I hooked a hand into Patrick's arm as a sign that walking suited me better.

"Thanks, Tony," he was saying. "We're going only one more block and want the walk. Where have you been all morning?"

The smile sickled into the plump cheeks. "Me? I went home and got some sleep. Sorry, Bud."

"All good detectives sleep, Tony. So long."

The little man leaned away from the wheel.

"Listen, Bud, don't you think I'd better stick around the Waldorf? Just in case. You know what's happened, don't you? They found that dame murdered. It's in all the papers."

"Well, maybe you had better stick around, Tony. Go back to the hotel now. We'll be seeing you after a while."

"I could take you where you're going now. And wait."

"Nope."

"Okay," Tony said. He seemed hurt.

The cab started and turned east before we got to the cross street. I asked Patrick if he honestly thought the taxi driver deserved the reward he'd suggested to Mr. Couch. He said if he wasn't one of the murder group he certainly deserved something for the way he kept sticking his neck out. If he was one, we'd find out, Patrick said. He looked pretty grim as he said it.

The nurse, Vivian Black, lived in a huge medium-priced hotel. We arrived at five minutes past the hour we had said to expect us. She was waiting in the lobby, dressed in navy-blue street clothes and looking exactly as you would expect a middle-aged nurse to look, in or out of uniform. She made up her mind to say nothing the minute Patrick explained why we had come. She showed genuine affection for the late Dr. Crossland. She openly hated his frivolous wife. If Mrs. Crossland had been the one to die the violent death I would have suspected Vivian Black. No, she declared, Dr. Crossland certainly had *not* been murdered. He'd been driven to suicide because he worked all day like a dog and his wife dragged him around all night. At their age! Imagine! Yes, case records had been kept on the Davison case. Dr. Crossland was strict about that sort of thing. Besides, Vivian Black had typed them. Her lips tightening, she then insisted that she never remembered a word she entered in any record. It was a nurse's job to keep the record, and to forget promptly what was in it.

Pressed, she seemed to remember that Brenda Davison suffered from migraine headaches. Lots of people did.

Her good-bye was as unfriendly as her original greeting.

"Well, that was a waste of good time," I said, outside again.

"On the contrary," Patrick said. He took my arm and we doubled back half a block to use a telephone in a drugstore. He tried first for the doctor he knew at Medical Center. He didn't reach him. Then he called our old friend Ellen Rawlings. I listened through the partly open door of the booth.

"Ellen, you used to be a nurse. Tell me something, is there any drug used for migraine which might make trouble for your corpuscles?"

"Heavens, Pat! I've no idea!"

"Brenda Davison suffered from migraines, didn't she?"

"Yes, I think so. I remember Anne's mentioning it."

"What about Katy?"

"Katy? You don't have migraines at that age, do you? Or do you? I do know that the child is rather subject to colds."

"And Anne gives her medicines, I suppose?"

"No. Brenda herself did that. She was sort of funny about it, according to Anne. It's all kind of hush-hush."

"You've heard about Brenda?"

"Yes. Isn't it horrible, Pat?"

"I'll say. Have you got a good doctor, Ellen?"

"A wonderful one. Why?"

"I want to know what drug or drugs might make bad trouble with your corpuscles. I've a hunch it's one given for migraine. Also, keep my asking it under your hat. And how about delivering this information to us Abbotts over a cocktail in the King Cole Room at the St. Regis one hour from now? Which will be around five o'clock."

"I'll be there. I don't know if I'll have the answer, though."

"Sure you will. Well, good-bye, Ellen. Be seeing you." He stepped out of the booth where I stood listening. He lit a cigarette. His eyes looked green and narrow. "Now we see the Ashbrooks. We'll find them at this hour, I think, in their rooms at the St. Regis."

"Did you make an appointment?"

"I certainly did not. Come along and don't ask any more questions. I'm thinking."

"But I hate to run in on people like the Ashbrooks without phoning first."

Patrick grinned and pulled my arm close.

"You'll never make a good detective, thank God. Incidentally, our friend Tony Konrad hasn't your delicate feelings. Don't look now, but he's nosing along behind us. We'll walk slow, so that he gets caught by a red light and while he's stuck we'll dash ahead and duck into the St. Regis before he catches up. Not that he won't suspect where we are, but at least that'll keep him guessing for a while."

15

Patrick said, "I must apologize for barging in on you without proper notice, Mrs. Ashbrook."

"Don't. I like people busting in. A detective's supposed to anyway, isn't he?" The foggy voice was cordial. "Besides, I hate being alone, even for the half hour it takes Clive to run down and get himself barbered. He'll be back soon."

We had got settled in the spacious living room of the hotel suite. The room was expensive-looking and charming. Its subdued tones became Elizabeth, who was quite glamorous in a trailing green-crepe dress with long sleeves and gold trimmings. She had had her red hair done, and the do was definitely smart. Her only jewel was a middle-sized emerald which, since it was coupled with a plain gold wedding ring, may have been her engagement ring. Emmerman? Or Ashbrook?

Her manner, indeed, was that of a woman who had recently been relieved of an overwhelming burden.

Aside from the small black poodle curled like a woolly lamb on a cushion in front of the wood fire and what Elizabeth had on her back, the magazine she was reading when we entered, a package of cigarettes and the long black holder, everything in the room belonged obviously to the hotel. Therefore I pictured Elizabeth Ashbrook as a woman who moved from one fine hotel to another accompanied by her husband, her luggage, and her dog. Would she move on again soon now? She loved Katy Davison. It was in her face for the most dumb to see when she was with the child, but how would a three-year-old fit into a life like hers? Did she really want her? That is, if Katy came without her money?

"I'm only just in myself," she said. "Twenty minutes or so. I had to take time out for repairs." She flourished a long white hand at her hair and there was a gleam of dark red nail enamel. "What we need is a Scotch. I'd've had one the minute I got here but I hate drinking alone. I hate doing anything alone. I know I don't look it, but I am a clinging vine. Now for the Scotch."

"None for me, thanks," I said.

"Oh, don't be mean, darling!" Elizabeth said, and in a moment she had reached for the telephone and asked for room service. She wanted a bottle of Haig and Haig, a syphon of soda, ice cubes, and four glasses. The pinch bottle? Yes, of course. "You two are a godsend! I was reduced to reading that *Vogue*, and the whole damn issue talks to its readers as if they are children of ten or morons. Paula Eastwood never makes that mistake. To Paula all clients, if they have dough enough, are knowing, witty women of the world. That's sense."

Patrick asked, "You didn't go up to Paula's place, did you?"

"Good grief, the place is crawling with policemen. Of course I didn't go. It wasn't necessary. Clive had to go again, to be quizzed about some nail polish. And the poor lamb is ignorant as possible about things like that. Besides, Brenda's name was on her special bottle. You'd think they suspected Clive, or something, the way they keep dragging him around to ask this question or that."

Her talk was airy. She was not worried.

"They suspect everybody," Patrick said.

"Me?"

"You, too. You gained something by her death, didn't you, Mrs. Ashbrook?"

"I expect so. I hope so, God knows—if you are referring to money. We live from hand to mouth. Worse than that. The sheriff literally dogs our heels. I do hope you two aren't the kind that blush when money is mentioned."

We laughed. What she said was nothing, but from her it was lusty and fresh. I could believe now too that her beauty twenty years ago was not mere legend. She looked ten years younger than last night.

"We're here because I want to know more about Paula Eastwood, Mrs. Ashbrook."

"Okay. But first there is something else, something very personal, which I'm saying because you two are so happy. I know it because I am too. I'm in love with my husband. He's wonderful to have around. He stimulates without boring me, he never makes unpleasant noises or breathes down your neck or stinks of lotions and things. And he loves me. That sounds so smug it's indecent, but it's the God's truth, and I'm saying it because people are eternally getting wrong notions about Clive. He's so handsome he's—well, it cripples him, if you know what I mean."

"Why are you telling me this, Mrs. Ashbrook?"

"You should know! The police act as though he killed Brenda. It's not even possible. He was constantly with me."

She started fitting a cigarette into the holder. Patrick got up to give her a light. Her hand was trembling!

"Why would he kill her?" Patrick asked.

"Why would any of us? For her money, of course." Her wide attractive mouth puckered up. "For *our* money, to be slightly accurate."

"Maybe we'd better talk about Brenda first. How much really do you know about her and her past?"

Elizabeth's almond-green eyes tightened a little.

"Nothing, save the various items she chose to disclose, many of which clashed."

"I take it you didn't like her?"

"I told you that. I'd often had the idea of putting a detective on her trail, that is, to dig up her past. But it always called for too much money."

I said, "She was beautiful. Pat could sit and gaze at her forever, I think."

Elizabeth laughed. "She was no menace as a woman," she said. "She hadn't one atom of sex appeal. I can't think why my brother Jack ever married her. He was a darling, just like Pete."

"Maybe she married him," I said.

"I like you better all the time," said Elizabeth. "Glory be, here come the drinks," she cheered then, as a waiter tapped and entered pushing a cart stocked with everything anyone associates with Scotch. "Now I'll feel human again," Elizabeth declared, after we were served and the man was gone. "It's wicked to be without Scotch. Isn't Katy a darling little moppet? I must say that Katy justifies Brenda, so why do I beef? Also I keep forgetting there isn't any longer any Brenda. Doubtless you're shocked."

"No," I said.

And I wasn't. And not because I knew there might still be a Brenda. The woman was natural as earth. She said what she thought, and since you yourself had had thoughts not too different from hers, you weren't shocked in the least. But I doubted if Lieutenant Dorn would agree with that.

Besides, if she had wanted Brenda out of the way what was to prevent her seeing that it was done? Not her conscience. She was amoral, maybe. And she knew it.

Patrick sat forward, his glass in one hand. "Tell me about Felix von Osterholz, Mrs. Ashbrook."

There was a faint tightening of the eyelids, a constriction of the muscles around the wide painted mouth.

Elizabeth then drained off her Scotch. She took it straight, and then sat sipping a glass of water.

Patrick said, "You know him, Mrs. Ashbrook. You didn't recognize him, though, till I read his name from his card."

Elizabeth's forefinger beat a light tattoo on the long black holder. Her hand wasn't shaking now.

"Odd, isn't it? We had one of those grand *affaires*. Don't be shocked, everybody knows it. Yet I didn't recognize him when he lay there on the floor. I hadn't even thought of him for years. That's what being happy does to you. Takes a lot of creases out of your brain or something. I ought to have known him by his eyebrows and his hair. And ten years ago I was insane because Felix wouldn't marry me."

"He must have been crazy," Patrick said.

"On the contrary. He was perfectly sane. I had by that time relatively little money. There was a Brazilian girl of twenty whose blood wasn't strictly Nordic but she brought Felix twenty million in cold cash. I wonder what's happened to her? I consoled myself with Clive and, my God, I fell in love with him. Please forgive my lapses in taste. They bother some people."

"Ashbrook didn't need twenty million?"

"Good heavens! Clive needs nothing, except me. You could put everything he owns in a couple of suitcases. People don't understand him at all."

"Can you tell me where to find von Osterholz, Mrs. Ashbrook?"

"No. I phoned everybody we mutually knew and I called all the hotels he would be likely to stay in, and then suddenly I realized that what I was doing was dreadful. I mean, possibly he's in this country illegally, and here I was, practically setting a trap."

"You wouldn't approve of his being here illegally?"

"Darling, it's not my affair. Besides, I wouldn't want to trap an old friend. Good Lord! Please drink up and let me pour you another."

My goodness! She was one of those people to whom the war meant only inconvenience, a separation from her friends, the loss of Paris for a while and other spots she liked. She did not think of the fighting, bloodshed, famine, and other horrors that stalked the earth because of people like Felix von Osterholz. Was he a Nazi? I asked it. She smiled and said he must have been since he was roaming freely around Europe at a time when all good Germans not Nazis were forced to stay inside Germany. Even that didn't bother her.

But I liked her all the same. She interested and amused me. She made me feel alive. She had guts. She offered the pinch-bottle. We declined, the original shots having been mammoth. She poured another for herself. Her color was rising. That weather-beaten look was coming back to her cheeks.

"I suppose you think I'm a stinker for not hating where I should? I'm a thoroughly selfish woman. I was glad that Clive was over age and couldn't be drafted. I discouraged his wanting to enlist. He speaks languages and could have been useful, I suppose. But I'm selfish. I want him with me. That's what money is for. To pay for what you want. I like to spend mine keeping Clive with me. He'd do the same if the income happened to be his."

I said, "Not all of us could keep our men with us, Mrs. Ashbrook. During the war."

She turned the wonderful green eyes on me.

"I said I was selfish. There's another reason, and I won't have you blabbing it around or crying over it in your Scotch. Hear? I have a ticker that ought, according to the doctors, have ceased suddenly to tick five years ago. So I said the hell with the war, I want him with me."

"I'm sorry. We didn't know about your heart, Mrs. Ashbrook."

She waved her hand at me, palm forward. "There you go! Forget it."

"Where did you know von Osterholz, Mrs. Ashbrook?"

"All over. Paris, Cannes, Salzburg, Rome. For years."

"Was he a Bavarian?"

"East Prussian."

"I wonder if he knew Paula Eastwood? In Europe?"

"I shouldn't wonder. She was a pretty thing, there in Vienna. She used to come and do me up in my hotel. Like as not Felix got acquainted then. He never could see the point to monogamy. None of his sort did."

"Paula entered this country as Paula Osterholz," Patrick said.

"Did she really? It's a good name where she came from. I dare say that's why she took it."

"Eastwood is one way of saying Osterholz in American."

Elizabeth's nod was casual.

"Of course. Funny, it never occurred to me, though."

"Will you describe her, please? I assume you're not averse to having her rounded up?"

Elizabeth laughed. "Not at all. She's a greedy devil and evidently a blood-thirsty bitch along with it. Well, she's a true ash-blonde. Her hair may be touched up. That was her specialty. My hair was ravishing when she tended it. Blue eyes. Very blue eyes, the delft shade, and hard balls of eyes they are, too. Protrude slightly, as if they are reaching out for your wad."

"Tall?"

"Medium. She had to diet to keep her weight down—a thing she didn't do in Vienna. She was plump there. The fattest thing about her lately is probably her bank account. Forgive me for harping on what I have already made too obvious."

"Any man on her string, Mrs. Ashbrook?"

"Why do you use the singular?"

"Von Osterholz, perhaps? Even if he's one of several."

The eyes shadowed.

"I couldn't even hazard a guess. Look, I feel such a dope, telling you about my silly pump. I don't know why I did it. Nobody knows I'm a dead ringer for a coronary almost any day except Clive and Hal Couch and my doctor. Pete suspects, but I've never told him."

"It won't go any further."

"That's why Clive hovers so. But I'd die, rather than have people think I'm ill. That's one thing about a heart. It at least doesn't give you that one-foot-in-the-grave look."

"Don't think about it, Mrs. Ashbrook."

"I want to live for his sake. Now, damn you, never mention the thing to me either. Do you hear?"

The door from the small anteroom of the suite opened and Clive Ashbrook came in. He was carefully dressed and groomed, but he did not look as if he had just come from the barber. He greeted us gravely. He shook hands. And, again, there was that faint unmistakable pressure which doesn't baffle any female over nine. I felt my color rising. I felt Elizabeth watching me, and, on looking at her when I was sure she had turned her eyes from me, for Clive was bending to kiss her cheek, I caught the tail end of a look which said plainly that Elizabeth wasn't half so sure about Clive as she pretended.

"We're talking about Felix," Elizabeth said to Clive.

Ashbrook helped himself to Scotch and soda and pulled up a chair.

"Have you heard any more about him, Liz?" His voice was deep and rich and even.

"No."

"The police are onto him, my dear."

Elizabeth's lips sagged. "How do you know?"

"They asked if I knew him. I had to say yes. They knew he was at Brenda's yesterday. I had to admit it, but I did say that neither of us would have recognized him. And of course we didn't know he was in this country without proper authority. They'll question you, darling. Tell them the truth."

"The truth? There's nothing to tell."

His rich voice deepened. "They will ask where you knew him. Tell them. Don't keep anything back. They think he's hooked up somehow with Paula Eastwood. The caretaker at that apartment house has seen him coming and going. The F.B.I. will be in this, too. We only knew him socially before the war. The war is over. So you've nothing to fear."

"But why did he kill Brenda?"

"Just what we thought. For her loot. The police think he and the Eastwood woman have also been up to a little blackmail." He said to Patrick, "I never liked the fellow much, to tell the truth. He was like a spoiled child. When he was happy he capered. When sad he sulked. All Germans are like that, in my opinion."

Elizabeth was again smiling.

"There you are. I thought Felix was a darling. Clive thinks Brenda was a pet."

Clive's smile was full of affection.

"She was so very beautiful, Liz."

"*Was*. I keep forgetting. Can't I offer you two some more Scotch?"

We again declined. Patrick said abruptly, "I've a notion that Paula Eastwood is dead."

There was a stillness. Elizabeth and Clive Ashbrook, two such contrasting people, both sat in the same sort of stony silence. Silence? It was fear. Their nostrils twitched. They waited.

"Brenda may be very much alive," Patrick said.

Glances whipped between them. Elizabeth's hand began to shake. She set down her glass. It quivered against the tabletop, making a succession of tiny clinks.

There was a strange shining in her eyes, as Clive said, "I beg your pardon. Mr. Couch and I had the unpleasant duty of identifying the body. I assure you it was dead. Very dead."

"You are positive it was Brenda?"

"Positive. The nail stuff. The hair."

Elizabeth shivered. The little fire made a hissing sound. The dog stirred and looked up at his mistress. It kept watching her as she reached for a cigarette. Her husband rose swiftly and got it for her. He stood fitting it into the holder. He took out his lighter and gave his wife the light as though the small effort would be too much for her.

"There is always hope," Patrick said. "Of course the police will do a complete autopsy and that should settle the question of identity. There may still be teeth enough to do the trick. They will analyze the hair. If it's Brenda's they'll know. They will make a blood test and check it at her doctor's. They will find out what she ate and drank last night, which will be fairly easy since she had dinner and spent the whole evening with Pete Davison and had a final coffee with us. A stomach analysis will take care of that."

"But that nail polish?" Elizabeth said. "That was strictly Brenda's. I disliked it intensely, but even I will admit it had chic."

Patrick's catlike attention was masked in diffidence.

"Anybody could have applied the polish after the woman was dead—if she isn't Brenda. Anybody can burn a place on the forearm and apply a Curity bandage patch, which was the kind that Brenda had put on herself. The police think the patch came out of the same box of bandages. That is, if the dead woman isn't Brenda. Who had access to the cabinet in Brenda's bathroom where the bandages are kept? The murderer hasn't a chance. He must be a fool or an idiot if he thinks in this day and age an identity can be destroyed by beating up the face. In these days of scientific investigation . . ."

From Elizabeth Ashbrook there came a sort of sigh. The dog got up and whimpered.

"God damn you!" Clive snarled at Patrick. His handsome face looked fiendish as he leaped to his wife's side.

Patrick also leaped. He was hanging onto her pulse by the time I came alive enough to get up and join the circle around Elizabeth. She lay softly in her chair corner. Her face looked gray. A faint, I thought.

A faint? I hoped!

"How dared you?" Ashbrook was growling. "She told you about her heart. Of all the god-damned carelessness . . ."

"And where were you while she was telling us that?" Patrick asked evenly.

"Now, see here. I wasn't listening. I just happened to . . ."

"Forget it. Get me some cold water and some towels."

"But . . ."

"Get moving!"

Ashbrook headed obediently toward what I supposed was the bedroom and bath. Patrick said that I was to count the other pulse. I picked up the wrist and rested my fingertips firmly where they would pick up the heartbeat. Even after all the Scotch the pulse came steady as a clock.

16

"Agranulocytosis," Patrick said. I said, "What-t?" He spelled it out. The long word annoyed me. Everything annoyed me, as a matter of fact. We were in a taxi—not Tony Konrad's—on our way back to Brenda Davison's apartment. Shadows were lengthening. The city went past in afternoon tones which were beginning to be blue. New York was relaxing a little, but me, I sat feeling tense and irritated, and all the time the feeling grew. First, Patrick had been rude to Ellen Rawlings. After she had bothered to find out about the many-syllabled disease he had asked us to wait a minute while he made a phone call. He was gone ten minutes. We had sat in the little lobby of the St. Regis waiting for him to come back. We saw Elizabeth and Clive Ashbrook come out of an elevator and walk out of the hotel. They didn't see us. He was clutching one of her elbows, but she walked with steady long steps as if she was well and healthy. She wore the mink coat over the long green dress. Very brief *heart attack*, I thought. I asked Ellen then if Elizabeth had a bad heart and she said she had lately heard that she had. I then asked questions about Clive Ashbrook and Ellen said he was apparently a fine chap.

"I think he had a mother complex," she said. "I think he grew up waiting on one charming, idle woman and it's quite normal for him to go on doing just that."

Oh. Maybe I roused the mother complex in him. The idea wasn't very satisfying, at that.

"Even those boys bust out now and then."

"I never heard of Clive doing it, Jean."

"How far would he go to make certain of future comfort?"

"I don't know him well enough to guess. I'm crazy about your hat."

It was a snub. But I said glumly that a flowery ribbony hat was a dilly to be chasing around in on a murder case, and that it was all I had, having sent all our things home yesterday by railway express because we expected to fly. Having had to give up our plane seats irritated me all over again. Then Patrick turned up and told Ellen we'd have to ask her to take a raincheck on the drink, because he was in a rush. "Unless you stay with Ellen, Jeanie?" he said, giving me a look which said he hoped to God I would, and I felt a sudden panic, which Ellen spied, because she said, too quickly, that it was too early for a drink and she'd be delighted to have it some time later. Any time.

Patrick told her, "It's the case. I've been talking with the police. The murdered woman was Paula Eastwood, not Brenda Davison."

"Oh," Ellen said. "What a relief!" she said then, but only in a polite sort of fashion, and I knew for certain that she did not much care for Brenda Davison. She said, "I never knew Paula Eastwood. Some of my friends used her shop, however. By the way, Anne Collier is anxious to see you, Pat. She wouldn't tell me why. She phoned twice."

"Is she at home?"

"Yes."

"We're going there now, Ellen."

"Have they found Brenda?" I asked.

Patrick shook his head. We left Ellen and, in the cab, he said, "The police theory has changed. Dorn now thinks Brenda is missing because she was mixed up in the murder of Paula Eastwood."

"Why?"

"The man. Felix von Osterholz."

"Have they got him then?"

"Nope. But they've learned that he had a way with the girls in the days before the war. Brenda denied ever having seen him before he had that fit in her place yesterday, but she hasn't much reputation for accuracy. Agranulocytosis."

"For heaven's sake!" I said, annoyed again.

"It's a disease."

"How nice!" I snapped. "How lovely!"

"It's a rare one."

"That's all right by me," I said, mad as possible, getting fussier every minute, even though I was ashamed of it.

Patrick was so pleased with himself that he almost purred. We were stopped by a red light at Lexington just then, and he said, "While you were with Ellen I called up a guy I know at Medical Center . . ."

"You said you called the police."

"I made two calls. The doctor at the hospital pieced out what Ellen had already told us about the disease."

"Then you needn't've bothered Ellen?"

"Look. I couldn't use what she'd told me without checking on it, could I? I tried to get this guy at Medical Center before I called Ellen. Now about the disease." The light changed and we moved up. "It occurs because of the reduction of certain types of corpuscles in the blood. The doctors don't know a lot about it yet. Only a few people are susceptible, so far as the doctors now know. These people remain susceptible all their lives to the things that cause it in themselves. One thing that can do it is pyramidon."

"Oh," I said, completely foggy now.

"Pyramidon is a common remedy for migraine headaches."

"Well?"

"Brenda Davison is subject to migraine."

"Is the what's-its-name serious?"

"Agranulocytosis? I say. It kills its victims pronto and with terrible pain. Unless the thing that causes it is spotted promptly, and stopped. But it's hard to diagnose and if death occurred it would almost be impossible to prove it was murder, if that was the means used. Now suppose somebody wanted to get rid of Brenda Davison in a way which would be hard to prove was murder. A few pyramidon tablets slipped into her aspirin bottle would do the trick."

"I take it they look like aspirin?"

"They do. Brenda wouldn't take pyramidon, of course. She'd know it would kill her. But if she would get one or two tablets accidentally—well, there you are. Only Dr. Crossland found out what was up—and there you are, too."

"Dr. Crossland committed suicide."

"Like hell he did."

"Now, wait—it was Katy who was sick. Not Brenda. I mean, when Dr. Campbell had to take over because Crossland was so suddenly dead."

"Right."

"You mean, Katy inherited this allergy?"

"It is not an allergy. And so far as the doctors know the susceptibility is not hereditary. It might however occur in two members of the same family. I asked my authority what he would think if it did. He said such an occurrence would be news and he would report it promptly to the American Medical Association and maybe do a paper about it. You may remember that Dr. Campbell thinks that Dr. Crossland may have had the case records of Brenda and Katy in his apartment and that the feather-brained Mrs. Crossland had let them get lost. I don't agree. I say that Crossland was murdered and the records stolen. I say he got in a state because Katy got pyramidon by mistake, which may have been how he discovered that she got the same reaction to the drug as her mother. I think maybe he started to investigate how the child got the pyramidon, and therefore got himself shot."

"You mean, the stuff was intended for Brenda?"

"I don't know."

"Can't you prove it, Pat?"

We were crossing Avenue A, and getting close to our destination. I could hear the traffic on the Queensborough Bridge.

"I cannot. I might as well go climb a tree. It happened three months ago. Crossland is dead. No case records. Katy's nurse has apparently vanished in thin air. Why? And where does Brenda herself fit in? Is she stark staring crazy, or what? Is she alive now or is she dead? Did she herself love the child, or even with Brenda was it only Katy's money?"

"Have the police any line on her at all?"

"Dorn said they'd thrown out a net. He said anybody as conspicuous as the black-browed auburn-haired von Osterholz and the *gladesome* Brenda couldn't hide away long."

"Dorn never said *gladesome.*"

"Right."

We pulled in at the curb. I said, "I wonder what happened to Tony Konrad?"

"Oh, the police have picked him up," Patrick said.

In the apartment the family was assembled in the living room. Sergeant Goldberg sat in the hall just outside, looking like Buddha might have looked if born in New York, and listening hard to every word spoken in the adjacent living room. The big room looked serene enough. The slats in the Venetian blinds had not been closed. Through them the afternoon sky shone blue and gold. The lamps in the corners had already been turned on. A coffee tray with extra cups and saucers was on the low table in front of Elizabeth Ashbrook. She seemed recovered from her heart attack, but the bloom which had given her the look of youth when we saw her at the St. Regis was gone.

She was pouring the coffee as we entered. Clive Ashbrook was handing the cups. Mr. Couch sat on the sofa with Elizabeth. Anne Collier, looking tall and defiant and intense, stood beside the hooded fireplace with her hands thrust into her jacket pockets. She refused the coffee with a sharp jerk of her straight tawny hair. Pete Davison was a bit away from the circle, seated at a place where he could watch Katy Davison, who was playing alone in the small adjoining study.

As Clive handed me coffee his dark eyes struck me for the first time as faintly shifty.

Elizabeth said to Anne, as if continuing some talk which had been going on when we entered, "But you are not the same kind, darling."

"Brenda and I have at least one quality in common, Liz," said Anne.

"What's that?"

"Neither of us would do murder."

Elizabeth's eyes quirked. "You seem very certain?"

"Very. I don't know what goes on. I don't know just why what we thought was Brenda turns out to be Paula Eastwood. But I'm positive Brenda had no part in it."

"She might have got roped in, somehow," said Clive.

"You refer to her bad company, I suppose? That's funny, too. Brenda declared all along she didn't know the people who kept crashing her parties. I believe her." Anne Collier's velvety black eyes looked directly into Elizabeth's. "I suppose after I say what I am about to you'll kick me out right away, Liz. I won't blame you."

"Then don't say it," Elizabeth said. "We certainly don't want to kick you out, darling."

"I'm going to say it. First I'm going to say it to you and then to the police. That's only fair. I'm not going to them behind your back. Here goes, then. You don't any of you like Brenda. You are all sorry it turned out to be Paula who was murdered. You were all happy as larks so long as the police thought it was Brenda. Now you're glum. You all act as if the joy had gone out of your lives."

"Now, really!" Clive Ashbrook said.

"You're all sitting here this minute hoping that the police have made a mistake and that it's Brenda, after all."

"Oh, Anne," said Mr. Couch.

"I don't mean you, Mr. Couch. You're merely tangled up with these lilies of the field. They're something you have to put up with, same as I, because you have to earn a living. Why, they're so smug and self-satisfied that they don't even realize what I'm saying."

Elizabeth smiled. "Even though you think me wicked don't put me down as dumb, dear. I do know what you mean. I don't like Brenda. That's the truth. But why must you stand there and lecture us because of that? We can't really help our dislikes, you know."

"I'm telling you off because I'm going to tell the police what I know about this set-up, but I don't think it's fair to tell them before I tell you."

I glanced at Pete Davison. He was watching Anne intently.

She hadn't made any exceptions. She'd linked him with Elizabeth and Clive. She was dressing down the whole lot at one time.

"You certainly have a low opinion of us, Anne," Clive said.

"I certainly do."

"If I may say so, what you're doing isn't the best taste . . ."

"The hell with taste! Look, this has gone a lot further than the bitchery which made you invite a lot of lousy people to this house, or have them invited. And things like that. One of you tried to murder Katy."

"Anne!" Elizabeth's froggy voice commanded.

The girl eyed her through narrowed lids. "It was you or Clive or Pete. Which?"

"Don't be primitive!" Elizabeth said.

"Have a heart, Baby!" Pete spoke up. "I wasn't even here then. . . ."

Anne pounced like a fiend. "And when exactly was the attempt made?" she asked Pete.

Mr. Couch leaned forward on the sofa. "Anne, if you got any such story from Brenda I—I should discount it, really."

"Hal doesn't like to say it," Elizabeth said, "but Brenda is a most accomplished liar, Anne. If she told you any such story about Katy, she lied."

"Rather," Clive Ashbrook said.

"She didn't tell me anything," Anne said. "I've got eyes and ears. They didn't have to be so super, either, to discover right at the start that Brenda was scared. In your fine spidery way you've kept her scared for years within an inch of her life. You never liked her. You resented her getting more of your disgusting money than you did. So you settled yourselves down to driving her slowly nuts. Well, you got what you wanted, didn't you? If she's not dead she is being suspected of murder. All you have to do now is to move in and take the kid and the money because you've shown she isn't fit to be Katy's mother any longer. But you've missed the bus. I can stop you and I'm going to do it."

"I don't suppose you'd permit me to say a word for myself?" Pete asked.

"There isn't anything to say. You're just like the rest. Instead of seeing what was going on you hung around long enough to see there was nothing in it for you personally, and then away you went."

"I didn't went, honey."

"Don't be cute."

"You win!" Pete's eyes were gleaming now. "Also, Baby, you've got to admit that Brenda is pretty much mixed up."

"Yes, of course," Mr. Couch said. "I wish you wouldn't talk about it now. Wait a little. Naturally, we're all upset. By tomorrow . . ."

"I am not upset," Anne said. "I've been thinking about speaking my mind for weeks. Then I'd get to thinking. I'd think, what's the use. I'm thinking that right now. Nobody can tell any of you anything because you're so damn smug nothing sinks in."

"Well, while you're airing our low natures," Elizabeth said, "why not enlighten us a bit on Brenda? Where has she been all her life? She had to grow up, you know, before she met and married Jack. Now, there's some information which I for one would be very happy to know."

"I know one place she wasn't," Anne said coldly. "She wasn't in Europe running with what's called the international set. Not giving a damn what happened to her own people or her own country so long as she had a good time. Only coming back here when it got uncomfortable there. I don't think Brenda had anything worse than that to cover up, Elizabeth."

"I suppose it depends on your viewpoint, darling."

Clive said, "But there must have been something odd in her past. . . ."

"Oh, cut it out!" Pete snapped. "If she's got a criminal record her fingerprints will be on file in Washington, and that will settle that. If she wants to be silent for personal reasons she's got a right to. I move this session be ended."

"Brenda was a snob," Elizabeth said. "Or *is*."

"You ought to know," said Pete.

"You mean, because I'm one? All right. Maybe it takes a snob to smell out another snob, and maybe I'm one and therefore I can spot it in Brenda."

"Sometimes I admire you," Anne said to Elizabeth.

"After all," Clive said, "we're not getting anywhere."

"I don't want to get anywhere," Anne said. "I just don't want you to say I didn't warn you. Brenda's in a tough spot. She has been, for a long time, ever since Jack was killed. She did not confide in me, but I hope I'm bright enough to spot misery and unhappiness when I see it. Brenda had a great deal of both. She is mixed up. She worries about the money. I think that Brenda had an unhappy childhood. I think she was poor, because otherwise she wouldn't always be thinking that to be poor is necessarily unhappy. Whatever else, I think it was just her bad luck that she landed in this awful family. You make me sick. The only thing that happened to any of you was relief when you found that Brenda was dead and now you'd have more money. Now she's alive and here you all are, back where you've always been, sulking, pretending—oh, the hell with it! Mr. Abbott, can I speak to you somewhere—somewhere . . ."

"Yes, rather," Patrick said.

17

Again the shadows lengthened and glamour descended on the East River. The water took on rainbow colors. The boats on the River turned black and began to bloom with red and green port and starboard lanterns. The heavy traffic of late afternoon growled from the bridge, and the wind blew up gently from the Bay.

I stood against the railing of the terrace having a cigarette with Pete Davison. Anne was giving Katy her supper. Patrick was downstairs in a heart-to-heart with Lieutenant Dorn.

Pete and I talked about the case.

"The trouble you made for yourself because you lied, Pete!" I said frankly. I said it because I wanted him to retract the lie. The sooner the better for everybody.

"Lied?" he said. Just as if he didn't know what I meant.

"You lied about what you did last night. The police know better. They've found out that your bag was checked in Grand Central Station all the time you say you made a trip upstate and then came right back again."

Pete was thoughtful. Then he said, "Well, that's so."

"What did you do during the time you said you were riding trains?"

"I was riding trains."

"But your bag?"

"It was in the station. That's the truth."

"But . . ."

"Look, the train was called, and I ran for it. I hadn't time to get my bag. I had checked it, meaning to wait for the next fast train, then this slow one was called and I made a dash for it. I was scared it would go off and leave me before I could pick up my bag. It's easy to send back for the bag, so what the hell?"

"Nobody will ever believe you."

"Do you?"

I said, "I don't know."

"I sort of thought you were for me, Jean." He sounded for the first time on the edge of resignation. I wondered if the police had been hard on him.

"I want to be," I said. "Only—only, you do such impossible things. You're crazy about Anne and you know it. Why don't you marry her, Pete? You're going to be miserable without her."

Pete stubbed out his cigarette and watched the dead end start its long fall into the river.

"She won't have me."

"I don't believe that, either."

"I do. You heard her just now? Well, that's how she feels. She says I'm one of them and in the long run I'll be just like them, so she isn't having any. She's a stubborn wench. She gave me the super-duper-de-luxe brush-off and no kidding."

"Try again," I said.

"I have. All day long. The police won't let me leave this place. But it's no go. And it's complicated because of the kid. I talked to Couch about that today. He was inclined to think that if Anne and I got married I might be able to have Katy."

"Did you tell that to Anne?"

"Certainly I did. I thought she'd be glad. I thought that would settle it, pronto. It made her simply furious, instead."

"Of course. She's terribly disturbed about Brenda. More than any of you, I think. She really likes Brenda."

"Well, anyway, now for some reason Anne thinks my wanting to marry her was part of a plan to get Katy and Katy's money. I don't give a damn about Katy's money. I want Katy. But, my God, you can't get rid of the money. The worst is that Anne doesn't believe anything I say."

I said, "Did you break the date with Anne last night, Pete?"

He wriggled. "Yes, I did."

"I thought so."

"I couldn't explain it to her at the time, Jean. Brenda was in a state. She phoned me. It started with the party, with all the people that she said were not invited, and that so-and-so passing out in the dining room. I was curious. I got the idea she knew the guy. I didn't see why she acted so damned scared unless she knew him maybe pretty well and was afraid the others would find it out. I wanted to talk to her and get the lowdown. So when she phoned me I said I'd take her out and then I called Anne. I didn't tell her why because Brenda didn't want her to know she was to see me. I thought I could fix it later. I . . . Okay, I'll tell the rest to Pat. He seems to be the doctor in this case, though, if you will excuse my frankness, he seems to be getting nowhere extra fast."

I said, "You never can tell. Things would be a lot easier for him, too, if all our clients didn't tell such lies. Even Anne lied. She said she broke the date with you herself."

"She did that to make it look better for Brenda. She likes Brenda. Of us all, only Hal Couch and Anne really like Brenda. I don't like her. I don't even feel sorry for her, I'm ashamed to say."

Well, neither did I, so I couldn't reproach him for that. I thought she was a silly woman, and in her way a sort of snob, if she got in a tizzy over what her in-laws thought about her, and tried to be somebody she wasn't.

"Couch likes her not as a girl or a friend but because she has business sense. He says she's young and that she'll snap out of this phase by and by and be all right. He says pretty drily that Brenda is the only one in the family who knows how to handle money. Of course, since his whole existence is a mess of fiscal statistics, he rates his clients accordingly. If Brenda runs a little wild socially Hal condones it because she's young and because he says that once you've got a good business head you'll always have it. But if she went wild enough to throw the Davison money around wildly, he would crack down on her pronto. He can't really forgive the rest of us because none of us have my father's business sense."

"He doesn't think Brenda a gold-digger, does he?"

Pete grinned. "He wouldn't hold that against her. And, honestly, I don't think she is one. She married Jack because she loved him. She could marry now at any time probably someone with a lot more money than the Davisons if she's a real gold-digger." Pete's grin was wry as he said, "Funny how we all talk about her now as though she is alive."

"Don't you think she is?"

"Sure, I don't know why, but I do."

I was aware suddenly of somebody else on the terrace and I glanced around and it was Patrick. He joined us.

"I've been scolding Pete for telling lies," I said.

"I was listening in," Patrick said. "Dorn wants you downstairs, Pete. He's out to get in his two cents' worth, by the way, and I don't think you'll find him easy."

"I don't expect to, considering the samples up to now." Pete stuck out his chin and stalked into Katy's sitting room. We watched him till he vanished into the upper hall.

"Pete admits leaving his bag in the checkroom," I said. "He says he dived for the train on the spur of the moment, thinking he could send back for the bag. It doesn't make too much sense. It was all so unthinking, I mean, running away and then running right back. But I believe him."

Patrick gave me a sidelong look. "People in love are crazy, according to Bernard Shaw."

"Well, they are. In a nice kind of way."

"Pete and Anne took out a marriage license five days ago. The police rooted that out this afternoon."

"Darling?"

"No wonder Anne feels touchy."

"Pete told me something else. He himself broke their date last night. He was worried about Katy, and Brenda had behaved so queerly that he wanted to spend the evening with her to see if he could spot what was up." I heard a step. "Shush, here comes Anne now."

Anne joined us by the railing. Even in the dusk her heavy hair gleamed like a drift of smooth dark gold.

"I made a proper show of myself downstairs a while ago, didn't I?" she said. "I don't suppose it will help Katy, either."

"How do you mean?"

"They'll get somebody else. They won't let me stay with her, after that. I should have had more sense."

"I can't say that what you said did any good," Patrick said. "But maybe it did no harm. Pete liked it, I think."

"Really," Anne said, coldly.

"Pete's all right," Pat said. "I think you are making a mistake there, Anne."

"That has nothing to do with—anything."

"Well, maybe not. Besides, it's off the beam at the moment. Ellen Rawlings said you had something to tell me?"

Anne said, "That was before they found out the body was not Brenda's."

"If you know anything you'd better tell it," Patrick said stiffly. "The body may not be Brenda's, but we don't know yet where she is or even if she is alive." He said, deliberately to prod her, "I don't quite get Brenda. I think from what I've seen of her that she isn't above doing things like disappearing for a day or two just to rouse interest in herself."

"You're just like all the rest," Anne said. Her voice was unsteady. I wanted to comfort her. But her attitude forbade comforting.

"Maybe. But I've got a job to find her, dead or alive. If you know anything at all that might help, speak up now."

Anne waited a moment, weighing it. "You won't pass it on?" she asked.

"Of course not."

"Well," she said slowly, "Brenda did know that Felix von Osterholz."

"I thought so all the time," Patrick said.

"Why?"

"Oh, little things. For one thing, by the way she reacted when he passed out. She was a little too positive about not knowing him, maybe."

"Liz didn't speak up, either," Anne said. She spoke in a low tone because she thought she was telling something we didn't know and she was ashamed of tattling.

"That was different," Patrick said. "Liz was once in love with von Osterholz. She is now in love with her husband and the realization that this man was once her lover, and that he was so changed she didn't recognize him, shocked her. Brenda was also shocked, but for a different reason. He wasn't supposed to show up at her party. But he did. Why? Why did he take a chance on upsetting Brenda, Anne?"

"Well, I'll tell you," Anne said. The light from the open door shone on her face. It looked drawn with worry. "He was trying to force a showdown. Brenda told me about it last evening, before she went out to dinner. She told me that she met him through Paula, her hairdresser, and that that was one reason she didn't dare let the others know she knew him. They'd say he was a fortune-hunter, too, she said, and that she wanted a title, and stuff like that. Also, he had written some letters."

"Letters?" I said.

Anne said, "That was why I phoned Ellen that I wanted to talk with you. The letters. I was having breakfast with Brenda when the first one came in. It was a funny handwriting. I saw it on the envelope and then on the closely written pages she was reading, though of course I never read the letters. I remembered it because she blushed so. She was pleased, too. There was another one the next day. The writing was the kind Germans use when they have first learned to write in German script."

"That's good detecting," Patrick said.

"No. I just happen to have had a correspondence with a German girl when I was in high school. You remember how we exchanged letters with people of all nationalities then? Well, this writing was like that. That is, cramped and packed on the page, as though it was necessary to save paper by writing lots of words to the line and lots of lines to the page. After the second one came Brenda never read them at the table. They came every day for a couple of weeks. Brenda kept them in a drawer of the small satinwood desk in her bedroom. One day they disappeared."

"She told you about it?"

"Not then. She was terribly worried, though. She asked me if I had seen anybody in her room. I hadn't, except the servants. But that made her suspicious of them. That is really why she put off their coming to live in the apartment. However, that wasn't fair, because everybody in that family has easy access to Brenda's room. They all come up here to see Katy. Brenda isn't always in. I'm out on this terrace with the kid. The servants are in the kitchen. Anybody can go in to her room and take anything."

"Why didn't Brenda keep the letters in her safe? Like her jewels?"

"That's what she wondered. After they were stolen. She couldn't understand being so careless."

"She told you about them, then?"

"She told me about them last evening. After the cocktail party. After he came here when she didn't invite him. She hadn't seen him for a month, not since he had written the letters. Last night Brenda decided that the letters were a put-up job. She already knew that he had been Liz's boy friend in Europe before the war. She was simply frantic. I suggested she talk with Pete. She was afraid to go to Mr. Couch because she knew he would scold her."

"So she went to Pete."

Anne's face stiffened. "She didn't have to. Pete called her. He broke a date with me saying that something terribly serious had come up, and then he dated her. That's what burns me up. The fact that neither of them told me. Then Pete spends the rest of the night behaving like the town's prize idiot."

Patrick said, "Anne, Pete is all right. Forget it. I understand you two took out a license to get married a few days ago?" Anne opened her eyes wide. "The police find out everything," Patrick said. "You go ahead and marry Pete. You won't make any mistake. Leave Brenda to me, and the police."

"But Brenda is swell!" Anne said.

"I hope you're right. But even you should admit she tries the patience. She gets so tangled up in her own lies. I'd never dare tell so many whoppers myself. You have to have such a wonderful memory to keep your stories all straight. Why didn't you tell me last night that she knew von Osterholz?"

"Why, I never thought of it, at first. I thought the others were right, that she had gone off with Pete. Then, after the body was identified as Brenda's, I didn't see any use in airing something they could be nasty about after she was dead. Then, after all, she's not dead maybe, and maybe I shouldn't've told it at all."

"Don't worry about it."

"But, does it help any?"

"It may. Do you think she might have gone out to her place at Sands Point?"

"Why—why, I don't know. She might."

"Does she always carry a key to that house?"

"I don't know. She keeps her keys in a little zippered suede pouch. I don't know if she would have that one in it now, or not. Besides, someone out there would see her. The place is on part of an estate. You have to be admitted through a gate. There's a gate-keeper."

"I know. Dorn says that the police checked with the gate-keeper this afternoon. He says she didn't come there. The place is on the Sound, isn't it? Has it a boat-landing?"

"Yes. But the house is closed, Pat. There's no water, no light, no heat or anything."

We went into Katy's sitting room and there among the small articles of furniture and the zebras on the chintz Patrick pulled out his map of Greater New York. It included one end of Long Island. With Anne's help he marked the spot where Brenda's house would be. Anne couldn't be very certain. She had been to the house herself only twice.

18

In the white glare of all the available electric light in the lower hall Lieutenant Jeffrey Dorn ran through some pencilled notes. He glanced up as we came down the stairs and his round blue eyes took on an expression of expectancy, as if he imagined Patrick might tell him something he was waiting to know. When he didn't, Dorn reluctantly passed on his newest item.

An answer had come from Berlin to a cable for information about Count Felix von Osterholz. The Count had been missing since the Battle of the Bulge, where presumably he had died in action at the head of his regiment.

"He's either in this country illegally, or he's a phony," Dorn said. "Either way he's in for trouble."

"How would he get here?" Patrick asked.

Dorn shrugged. "They still manage it. You know that. They get to Mexico or Cuba. Then sneak in here. I understand from Ashbrook that Osterholz is a linguist. Maybe he walked out on his men in Belgium and made it into France, or Spain, and under an assumed name shipped out as a deckhand or something." Dorn was tired and jumpy. "Anyhow, it's just that much more trouble for me. I'm going home for a while. You've got my phone number. You can reach me there if anything turns up. Sure you've not got any new ideas?"

"None worth mentioning."

"Any fresh slant on where Brenda Davison might be?"

"I've told you every time you've asked that that I'm not organized to find missing persons. That's police work. New York has the best police force in the world, Lieutenant Dorn."

"Right," Dorn agreed, perking up. "The trouble is, that woman lied so much. She told the family she came from a place called Liberty, in Illinois. They've never heard of her there. She appeared suddenly in Chicago when—according to her story—she was eighteen. From there on she's on record. She registered as Brenda Westmore at a well-known business school. She did all right. She got a good job right out of school. The second job she got was as private secretary to Jack Davison, and she married him. During the time she was in Chicago she lived at the Y.W.C.A. She behaved herself there, too."

"Good work," Patrick said.

Dorn's chest swelled visibly.

"Routine. Beyond that there's nothing. Where was she all her life before she was eighteen?"

"No criminal record?"

"Nothing has turned up," Dorn said.

"Brenda Westmore," Patrick repeated. "No doubt an assumed name."

"Right." The lieutenant dropped his voice. "The estate's agent, Couch, knows more than he's telling. He admits it, but insists that until she is proved dead he is not free to tell us what he knows. He does say that she came from a respectable, but poor, family, and that they are not in Illinois. I'll put the heat on him tomorrow if she hasn't shown up. Nobody ever knows as much about a person as the man who handles that person's money."

Patrick nodded. "By the way, what did you do about Tony Konrad? I meant to ask that before."

"One of our men picked him up. Konrad was tailing you, see, and the operative thought his actions suspicious. The fellow's either very smart or he's goofy. I incline to the latter view. We're on his tail."

"You told me you wouldn't bother him, Dorn."

"It wasn't my fault. The operative wasn't informed. Konrad's a perfect nuisance."

"No harm done," Patrick said. "Keep an eye on Tony, if you can manage it. I suspect he's heading for trouble."

Dorn frowned. "The nuts are the worst. So long."

Patrick asked Dorn as he started away if he could get him a gun. The lieutenant handed over his own Colt revolver, saying he'd pick up another.

Sergeant Goldberg was still hovering outside the entrance to the living room. There, in the soft glow of electric lamps, the Ashbrooks and Mr. Couch sat waiting. Whisky and soda had replaced the coffee on the table in front of the sofa. Elizabeth's face had taken on high color. It wasn't hard now to guess its habitual cause. Clive looked sullen. Mr. Couch looked tired. His face was gray from fatigue.

"Hello, kids," Liz greeted us. "We're waiting for your orders, Detective Abbott."

"In that case, Mrs. Ashbrook, I'd suggest that you go along and have dinner and relax."

"Nothing new?" Mr. Couch asked.

"Nothing worth mentioning. I've got a hunch Brenda may have gone to her place on Long Island."

The Ashbrooks exchanged glances.

"I shouldn't think so," Clive said. He sounded almost hostile.

"It's an ungodly cold damp place without heat," Elizabeth said. "Brenda doesn't like discomfort, you know. Whatever else, she's not *fin de siècle.*"

"Still, it's worth looking into," Mr. Couch said. "The gate-keeper there might know something. You could phone him, perhaps."

"He's been questioned already by the police," Patrick said. "He's seen no one. There's been no light noticed in the house. But I think I'll go out there, after dinner."

Ashbrook frowned. I wondered why I had thought him so handsome. Now he seemed ugly, almost repulsive. "If I may say so, Abbott, you seem very casual?"

"Why?" Patrick said. He sounded very casual.

Clive stood up.

"You say you think you'll go out there after dinner? Things like that. Why not go now?"

Patrick relaxed, like a cowboy getting set for action.

"Because it's only a hunch. I haven't got a seeing-eye, Ashbrook. I can't spot Brenda Davison in a whole cityful of seven million people."

"If I may say so," Clive Ashbrook said, "I can't see that you've made any real progress. And Hal and Elizabeth agree with me."

Mr. Couch said, "Now, Clive. Don't be hasty. I didn't say Mr. Abbott hadn't made any progress. I said the police were covering the case very thoroughly. I told you that I would not have incurred the extra expense for the estate had I known how efficient one of our Homicide Squads could be."

"Well, why not do something about it now," Elizabeth said. She didn't even look at us. She was through with us. She no longer troubled to please us.

Mr. Couch said, "You make things hard for me, Liz."

Patrick lit a cigarette. "You're too late," he said.

Clive moved a step toward us.

"If we are dissatisfied with your services we can sack you, Abbott. Or know the reason why."

"You're not paying me anything personally," Patrick drawled. "I'm in this on my own. I asked that any compensation take the form of a reward. Even that may not be called for. If I choose to smoke out a few rats on my own hook and at my own expense that's up to me, so long as the police don't stop me. Even if they tried maybe I'd go ahead and do it anyway."

"If you're really serious, why not leave your wife out of it, Abbott?" Clive said, nastily.

Patrick flicked off an ash. He did not bother to reply.

Mr. Couch rose. "We're all tired and worried. This has been a great strain. I am going to take Mr. Abbott's advice and go home and go to bed. If there is anything to do, Mr. Abbott, that's where you can find me." He handed Patrick a card with both his home and business telephones on it, and started out to get his overcoat and hat.

"But he's not getting anywhere!" Ashbrook persisted.

"I expect that's hard to tell, Clive," Mr. Couch said. "Why don't you two come with me? I'll drop you at your hotel."

We went down in the elevator with the Ashbrooks and Mr. Couch. They went off in a cab which had just pulled up to let out a fare. We chose to walk.

"Fine bunch," I said. "Mr. Couch, too. Trying to give you the brush-off, after all you've gone through!"

"Mr. Couch does what his clients want. That's the trouble with being an agent."

"I feel let down," I said. "I thought Liz was better stuff."

"Liz has her own game to play, Jeanie. And she knows we know she hasn't a weak heart."

"I wonder why she pretends it? Specially when she declares that nobody knows it except a couple of other people."

"Don't ask me. But I've got an idea."

"What?"

"She's worried that Clive will leave her. That heart keeps him dancing attendance. After all, he wants her to live. She may not be the super de-luxe meal ticket he counted on, but there may be no better prospect at the moment. Liz is smarter than Clive. No doubt she keeps a jump ahead of him all the time."

"Do you think he made passes at Brenda?"

"I don't know. I think Brenda wouldn't discourage it if he did. It would be one way to even things with Liz. Brenda really is smart in some ways. She's got them all guessing."

"All but Pete."

Patrick slanted me a look in the dark. "Why not Pete?"

"He's got her sized up, Pat. Pete's smart."

"Maybe. But he's playing a cockeyed game."

"What do you mean, game?"

"Maybe it's not a game. I'm not pressing Pete. And he certainly is giving out nothing, voluntarily. The police make him tell his story about taking the train over and over. He never misses. But he goes very light on details. That's clever. Brenda would have overdone her story and afterwards got tripped up on the frills. Maybe Pete's the best liar of the whole bunch."

"I just can't see it."

"I'm sure that Pete knew something was up last night. He didn't even trust Anne with what he knew. Anne's too loyal to Brenda. I frankly don't know just what his angle is. I like him. I think he's all right. I wouldn't've said so to Anne if I hadn't. But so far there is not one thing I've noticed in Pete Davison that rates him as a boy who would blindly hop one train and hop off and grab another back to town when things were so tense in his family."

"What do you think he did, then?"

"I think he checked out of the hotel and went to the station, checked his bag and then went sleuthing on his own hook. He wanted to appear to have left town. Maybe he told Brenda he was leaving. I don't know what he found out. I haven't yet figured out a way to get it out of him either. Also, it's not the time. He belongs to the police at the moment. The police have got him cooped up in that penthouse, making him tell his train story over and over and taking it down in shorthand every time."

"Darling, I thought you liked Pete."

"This is a murder case," Patrick said.

"But Brenda isn't murdered. At least, for sure."

"Dr. Amos Crossland was murdered. Katy Davison might have been. Paula Eastwood, a greedy bitch or what have you, is horribly dead. If Pete Davison knows something pertinent and doesn't speak up I don't give a damn who works at sweating the truth out of him."

"Oh, dear," I said. I felt sunk.

We crossed Avenue A on the green light. I felt really awful. I wanted Pete and Anne out of it, clearly and completely.

They were in love.

We walked on half a block.

"Psst!" somebody hissed. I clutched Patrick's arm.

A cab slid in to the curb just ahead of us. Its flag was down. I watched it warily as we came alongside.

"Hey, there, Bud?"

Tony Konrad again. My blood ran cold.

Anyway, Patrick had that gun.

Tony popped out of the cab and put one hand on the handle of the rear door. He was beaming with success.

"This sure is luck, Pat. Look inside."

Tony opened the door. Patrick flicked his lighter to illuminate the interior and we both peered in.

In the cab sat Brenda Davison.

19

In a Spanish restaurant we'd found on Bleecker Street and which Brenda thought sufficiently off the Davison beat to be safe from discovery she wolfed vegetable soup and *arroz con pollo* like one long starved. She did not look, however, as though she'd been out of polite circulation for even a few hours. She looked very neat. She was dressed in the bluish tweed suit which Anne had said was missing from her wardrobe. On the banquette beside her lay the evening bag glistening with its paillettes. Her silvery-blonde hair was concealed under a thin white scarf.

The cinnamon-red nail polish was undimmed and unchipped by whatever had happened since her disappearance in the night. It must have been a ladylike experience.

Me, I was jealous! It was no use. I could not shake it off.

We asked no questions at first. She must eat, Patrick said, and then talk.

The restaurant occupied a long narrow room with a bar at the front and the street-entrance opening cornerwise opposite the bar. The bar, of course, was the place's heart and chief ornament. Between it and the entrance was an open space. We sat in beside the open space in the first of a series of booths. Behind us, opposite the bar and between us and the entrance, was an immense juke box. A sailor occupying a bar stool kept feeding the box nickels to play his favorite songs. His very favorite was Frances Langford singing "Night and Day." The bartender was also the proprietor. He had a huge Spanish hatchet face and small black watchful eyes. Among his clients at the bar was a flock of young fiery-eyed dowdy-looking talkative Villagers, and a middle-aged blonde woman dressed in leopard-skin slacks, a lot of junk jewelry, and a short green flannel jacket. Her plump bald companion looked like a clerk. The leopard woman ignored her escort because the kids around her were more fun, and because the plump little man was blissfully drunk. When not mixing drinks the bartender usually watched the blissful plump man.

A huge poster on the mirror behind the bar said Our Country Right or Wrong.

Our waiter, a Latin and presumably Spanish, hovered around us to gaze at Brenda Davison. She seemed quite unaware of it. The real test of her perfection was her unconsciousness of it. She had none of the facial mannerisms which spoil beauty, no twistings and simperings and such.

She had a cigarette with her black coffee but refused a liqueur. "Now tell us what happened," Patrick then said.

She answered without hesitation, accompanied dolefully by "Night and Day."

"A man came into my room. He had a gun. He ordered me to get dressed and to bring all my jewels. I put them in this bag." She wagged a finger at the drawstring bag. "What wouldn't go in he put in his pockets. We left the apartment. We went out the front door, then the man walked me back to the service elevator. The front way, he said, was too risky. Down below, at the landing, was another man with a boat. It was my own launch from my place on Long Island, but I didn't know that then. I was told to get in the boat. I was absolutely paralyzed with fear. I thought they would throw me out of the boat somewhere. But they took me directly, in the boat, to my house at Sands Point and left me there alone."

"How were you dressed?" Patrick asked. I remembered that it had been rather hazy close to the river last night. Her suit did not look as if it had had any rough or even damp going. In fact, she looked entirely neat. Her lip rouge—in harmony with her nails, but not the same shade—was carefully put on. Her eyebrows looked brushed. Her complexion was natural all the time, and while a bit pinker than yesterday not at all roughened by exposure to weather.

The faraway innocent expression of her eyes never altered.

"They had a slicker for me, and a fisherman's hat. They had rugs. I was frightened, but really not uncomfortable. The boat is a good one and the man who piloted it knew how to navigate."

"Did you recognize the man?"

"No."

"Neither of them?"

"No."

"How did you get into that house?"

"I had my key. I have one always on my key ring. The one who came into my room made sure of that, but I didn't know why then. I thought he thought there was something worth stealing in that house. I tried to think of a way to warn Anne. The best I could do was to drop a glove on the boat-landing."

"Paula Eastwood's place is near the river," Patrick said. "It was assumed when the glove turned up that you'd been taken there, by boat."

Brenda seemed puzzled.

"Why there?"

"It was merely one theory. Go on."

"That's about all there is, really. The men seemed to know all about me. They knew I'd been out all evening. They waited until I'd gone to bed. I was reading, as I do just before going off to sleep. Suddenly the door opened and the man stepped in. I was too startled to scream, even."

"Were both in the apartment?"

"No, one waited below with the boat."

"How did the one get in the apartment?"

"He must have been in it when I got home. I put the chain on the front door when I locked it for the night. I always do."

"Then whoever engineered the plan knew you'd be out late and that the chain would probably not be on till you came in."

"Yes. I think so."

"Who would know that?"

"Anyone who knew I was out would know it. They'd know I wouldn't ring and wake Katy."

"Anybody phone you, after you came home?"

Brenda put both hands on her cheeks and pressed the smooth flesh with her cinnamon-enameled fingertips. Not a broken nail, not a fleck of polish was missing. I did not believe a word she said. My feeling about her was cold and merciless.

Still, I stayed jealous.

"Yes. After I got into my room, after I had told Anne good night, my private phone rang. It buzzes, so as not to make unnecessary noise. It was— Clive Ashbrook."

"Why do you have an unlisted phone?" I asked. Why would she need it? She wasn't a prominent person, needing the privacy an unlisted phone gives.

She said, "I wanted it."

"How did Ashbrook know your private number?" Patrick asked, after giving me a nudge.

"They all know it."

"Does Ashbrook often call you?"

"He never calls me." But Brenda blushed. "He sometimes gives you one of his looks or squeezes your hand, but he hasn't got the nerve to try anything, really. He called me last night because . . ."

The waiter was hovering again, to gaze on Brenda, vocally to ask to serve more coffee. He took his time.

At the bar the tipsy plump man teetered on his stool. The sailor sauntered over to the juke box, studied its repertoire, and again put his nickel on "Night and Day."

"Go on," Patrick said.

Brenda ran her tongue over her lips. "Clive wanted to know how I happened to know Felix von Osterholz."

"You told him?"

"Why, naturally. I said I'd met him some time ago through Paula East-wood. I was sorry right away I'd told him that. Clive isn't as sweet as he looks. He asked me if Liz had been seeing the bastard at my house. I'm quoting Clive—oh, I suppose I shouldn't've told that?"

"Of course you should," Patrick said.

"I—I hadn't told them about Felix because I knew that he and Liz had an affair which lasted years, in Europe before the war. I think Liz never got over him. Clive knows it. He's jealous of Liz, frightfully."

"Yet he plays around?"

Brenda shook her head. "I think—as I just said—he makes a few eyes and presses hands to let you know there's life in the old boy yet. And that's all." She smiled a little. "I think he doesn't care to risk his luck."

"Then, after Ashbrook phoned, the man came into your room?"

Brenda nodded. "But he must have been in the apartment while I was talking? I had put the chain on the front door before Clive phoned."

"Was there one on the kitchen door at that time?"

"Well, no."

"The elevator man had a pass key, didn't he?"

"Oh, yes. Maybe that's it. Oh, I don't think Clive had anything to do with the burglars. I think they wanted my jewels."

"Rather elaborate way to get the stuff, Mrs. Davison. A real burglar would take the loot and beat it."

"I don't know. Anyway, they ended by taking it, Mr. Abbott."

"All those important-looking stones?" I cried.

Brenda said, "It doesn't really matter. They were imitations."

"Oh?" I said. My goodness!

"The insurance was so terrific, I finally decided to have everything copied. I keep the originals at Cartier's. Nobody knew that, of course."

"Nobody?"

"No. Not even the insurance people. I just dropped that, without telling them anything. It wouldn't be any fun to wear the stuff if people knew it wasn't real."

"No, it wouldn't," I said.

She never looked at me at all. Not even when I got a word in. Forever Brenda, though behaving on the whole very well.

"What happened when you arrived at your house on Sands Point?" Patrick asked.

"Oh. They tied the boat to the landing and took my key and opened the house. One of them knew his way around, though I'd never seen him before in my life."

"Has Osterholz ever been in that house?"

"No-o. It's been closed all winter. I didn't know Felix until shortly before Christmas."

"All right. Go on."

"They took me upstairs. On one side the water comes in pretty close at high tide, and there's a whole mass of rocks. They put me in a room on that side, one which I use as a guest room. It has a bath, but no exit except the hall door which is also its entrance. There were blankets in the clothes closet. They left me and locked the door on the outside. They had left the slicker and robes they'd given me in the boat. I wrapped myself in blankets and sat down in a chair. I felt stunned. Pretty soon one of them came up with a thermos full of hot coffee they'd made in the kitchen. They'd got the water from a kettle, they said. He unlocked the door, brought it to me, went out, and that was the last I saw of them. It was dark but I peered through the blinds and I made out the boat as they started it going and chugged away."

"Very considerate, weren't they?" Patrick asked. "The coffee and blankets and so on, I mean."

An imploring expression filled her eyes. "I don't expect you to believe me, really. But it's true."

"Weren't you scared?" I asked.

"Oh, I was petrified with fear. I knew they'd find out the jewelry was imitation when they got back to New York. Then they would come back. But the late hour was in my favor. It was already close to daylight when they left. They would have to wait till night to get back again without being seen. I thought up a way to escape. The windows weren't sealed on the outside. When daylight came I would drop out. I'd have to light on sand, or break a leg, so I didn't dare try it in the dark. And then—I am ashamed to tell this because I'm afraid you won't believe it—I went to sleep."

"Why not?" Patrick said. "Sleep comes naturally in moments of intense fear. It's one of nature's safety valves."

She smiled happily at such understanding, and inside I seethed, thinking how blindly Patrick believed her.

"I was awakened by a loud noise somewhere in the house. I thought I dreamed it, though, because I heard nothing more. It was almost dawn. I got up and looked out a crack in the blind. The tide was coming in! It was running fast and already it was covering some of the rocks under the window. I didn't dare jump. I had to wait now for the tide to go out. There was still coffee in the thermos, so I drank it and wrapped the blankets around me and waited. I waited and waited. The tide went out and there didn't seem to be a good place to jump. I kept waiting. I hate to tell you what a coward I was, because I waited till dusk and the tide was coming in again when I finally got the nerve up to throw the blankets down and drop on them. I picked them up and left them on the side of the house away from the water and made my way to the station."

"Did you see the gate-keeper?"

"Oh, no. I didn't want to be asked questions. I walked along the shore to a place where a public lane comes down to a small beach, walked along the lane to the highway, and got a ride to the station. I was lucky and got an express to New York almost at once."

The taxi driver, Tony Konrad, came into the restaurant. He strolled across the open space to the bar, got a packet of matches from the hatchet-faced proprietor, looked at us, flapped an arm like a fin, and strolled out. Brenda said, "You know, somewhere, I've seen that man before."

Patrick said, "Sure. He brought us here. He's waiting outside."

I said, "He's appointed himself our chaperone, Mrs. Davison."

"I don't mean tonight," Brenda said. "I mean, before tonight, somewhere."

Patrick said, "You say you took a train. Did they leave you money?"

"There was a little in my change purse. My make-up was in my bag, too. I made myself as presentable as I could before leaving the house."

Very smooth, I thought. Too smooth. Pretty soon she'll tell us that her abductors served up bacon and eggs and toast. Buttered.

"Did the men ever come back to the house?" I asked.

"Not while I was there, thank goodness."

"But that loud noise?"

"Oh, I'm sure I dreamed that."

She was lying! Again there was that airy note, that overtone from the lie, just like last night when she was talking about her lovely family. She was hiding something.

Patrick said, "The police will check very closely on your story, Mrs. Davison. They'll go to that house. They'll check to see if you really jumped from the window."

"How can they tell? The tide will have been in and out again before morning."

"They have ways. How did you happen to get into Tony Konrad's cab after you got back to New York?"

"He came up to me outside the Waldorf. When I got to Penn Station I decided not to go home but to come to you. I took a cab. When I got out and started into the hotel this Tony Konrad popped up and said he would take me to you. He said maybe you were at my apartment. I was suspicious but I didn't want to make a fuss. I asked him how he knew me and he said my picture was all over New York, in the papers, he meant, which was the first time I knew there was any excitement. That upset me. I wanted what seclusion the cab could give. In the cab he told me I was supposed to have been murdered."

"Not you," Patrick said, very, very gently. "Paula Eastwood."

There was a silence. Brenda stared. She sat like something in wax. Stiffly her fingers reached for her little coffee cup. It jittered in its saucer as they touched it. She let it stay where it was. The adoring waiter flew to see what was wrong. Ah, the coffee was cold? He must fetch more. He whisked away all our cups. He danced off, promising fresh cups, fresh hot coffee. The bartender left the bar and with great consideration escorted the blissful bald drunk out onto the sidewalk. He came in and signaled a waiter to take his place at the bar for a while and went off toward the kitchen at the rear. The sailor spent another nickel on "Night and Day." The aging Bohemian gal in the leopard-skin slacks watched the exodus of her escort and went on sipping her drink.

Having been given a little time, Brenda looked composed again, when she asked, "What about Paula Eastwood?"

"She was murdered. Last night. About the time you were found to be missing."

"How did that happen?"

"Anne heard the front door close, got up, and discovered you were gone. She was frightened, and sent for me."

"I mean—*Paula*."

"Paula was killed with an andiron. Her face was beaten beyond recognition, and because she was left naked and her hair is like yours and because she had a small Curity bandage patch covering a slight burn on one wrist she was identified as you."

Brenda's fingers went to her coat sleeve. She slipped it up and there was that small adhesive patch on her wrist.

Patrick said, "Also, her nail enamel was like yours."

"She used a very different shade," Brenda said.

"Your enamel had been put on after she was dead."

Brenda trembled. "Who—who identified her?"

"Clive Ashbrook and Mr. Couch. Anybody would have mistaken her for you, Mrs. Davison, specially after one of your gloves was found in the apartment. How did that glove, which is a mate to the one found on the landing, get into Paula Eastwood's apartment?"

"But how would I know?"

Patrick cut in, his voice low and full of authority.

"The police are going to ask you a lot of questions. When I was a boy my mother taught me that the truth itself is not believed from one who often has deceived. I'm afraid you didn't learn that maxim, Mrs. Davison? Perhaps you had no mother?"

"No," Brenda said.

"You will have to tell the police about that, too, I'm afraid. You can skip it

with me at the moment. Other things are more urgent. First, how can we find
Felix von Osterholz?"

"But . . ."

"Answer quickly, please."

"But, I don't know. Paula knew, but if . . ."

"She's dead. You met him through Paula?"

"Yes-s."

"You fell for him, didn't you?"

She flushed. "A little. I soon got over it."

"Why?"

"Well—well, he dyed his hair, for one thing. When I found that out he
seemed—well, ridiculous."

"Also his eyebrows?"

"I don't know. Why would anybody want such great black eyebrows?"

"Why would anyone want to dye his hair? Unless he was an actor? I understand he wrote wonderful letters?"

Brenda turned pale. "Oh. How . . .?"

"Never mind how. Did you answer them?"

"Oh, no, for heaven's sake! I should have burned those letters. They were
stolen. They were all part of a plot. They have been trying all along to get rid
of me. They want Katy's money. They think . . ."

"Which one is it?"

Brenda spoke with bitterness. "All of them. I haven't a chance. No matter
what I do they will make it seem something disreputable. There is that will."

"Hoo-ey! Such wills are made to be broken. They never stand up in the
showdown."

"But they are both against me. They gang up. Pete doesn't like me any
better than Liz."

"You told me Pete asked you to marry him?"

Her eyelids flickered, then she said, "That wasn't true. I asked him. He
turned me down. I—I didn't want to admit it."

"Are you in love with him?"

"Of course not."

"Didn't you know he was in love with Anne Collier?"

Her face was wondering. "No. No, I didn't."

Of course she didn't, I thought. She is too self-centered to realize anything
unless it concerns herself.

"You knew, didn't you, that von Osterholz isn't really von Osterholz?"

You would have sworn her astonishment was genuine.

"But he must have been? He . . . You see, he knew Liz . . . He was—he
was . . ."

"Her lover for years?"

Brenda colored. "I wasn't going to say it."

"You might as well. Everybody knows it, but there are more important things than that. We've got to find him. We want to know who killed Dr. Crossland. Who planted the drug among your aspirin tablets and almost killed your little daughter. Who killed Paula Eastwood because she knew too much. I personally want to know if you have been telling me the truth. You've got to prove it. To start with, we're going out to that house of yours at Sands Point and you're going to show me . . ."

"No!" Brenda cried. "No, no, no!"

20

There followed one of the soft-tongued flattenings-out my husband does so thoroughly when he finally gets around to it. Without lifting his voice, with no gestures, with very little of the spicy language he uses at times so effectively, he sat there and kicked Brenda Davison's lovely teeth in. He said his chief regret was that he couldn't beat her up as she deserved. He said he'd been charmed by her Renaissance face but that frankly speaking the Renaissance brain behind it stank. Sprawled at ease on the uncomfortable banquette, smoking lazily, his eyes narrow, his face never changing, he called her a liar and a coward. She hadn't any guts. So what therefore gave? Pete Davison was on the spot. The Ashbrooks were under deep suspicion. Old Mr. Couch was in a tizzy, dangerous at his age. Dr. Crossland was dead. Paula Eastwood was dead. Felix von Osterholz was currently unaccounted for. And little Katy Davison herself was in constant danger, and it was all because of Brenda's lies.

"And what is your motive behind it all?" he asked her. "Your incredible silliness and vanity, of course, but what else?"

Like a surrealist background was the bar with the hatchety bartender, the old would-be Bohemian in the leopard pants, the tipsy Village poets and poetesses, the rainbow-hued jukebox droning "Night and Day," the smells of gin, whisky and spicy Spanish cookery.

"When I get finished with you," Patrick said, "I'll turn you over to the police and they'll sweat the truth out of you, if it can still be done."

Brenda took it. She did not cry. Her lips trembled, but she attempted no defense. Patrick apparently got nowhere very fast.

I think I felt worse than she. I felt wretched. I hated his pitching into her like that. Though I was still jealous.

The girl had had a hard time, whatever else. Yet she did look so tidy. There was a little dark stain on one sleeve I hadn't noticed at first, but otherwise she was trim as a pin.

The adoring waiter hovered until Patrick fished out a bill and sent him to a drugstore across the street for the best pocketsize flashlight he could buy. When he came back Patrick tipped him flatly and gestured him out of the way. He deserted Brenda and removed himself to a place near the bar.

"We're wasting time," Patrick said then. He hailed the waiter, paid the check, and again over-tipped. "We're going now to your house at Sands Point, Mrs. Davison."

"But why?"

"You've got to prove you really stayed in that house last night—what remained of it—and today."

"But—but how could we get in? They took the key."

"We'll get in." That part would be easy. Locks aren't much trouble to an experienced detective. "You're smart, Mrs. Davison. You're too smart. And not smart enough. Super-smart people don't tell useless lies."

"But—but—if it's about myself—before . . ."

"All right. Tell it. And make it snappy."

This time her parents had died when she was three years old and she had grown up with a grasping aunt, whom she hated. She ran away when she was eighteen and came into a little money her parents had saved for her education. She had sent the aunt fifty dollars a month ever since she'd started working, advising her that she would stop it if the aunt ever tried to make contact with her.

"I hated her!" she said. And she sounded authentic. It was no use. I didn't believe her, just the same.

"Her address?" Patrick demanded.

"Oh—please . . .!"

"It won't be used unless necessary. The police think you've got a criminal record, because you're covering up your past. If they find out you have, we won't need to bother with that address. Come on. Give!"

"How absurd!"

"The address. And your name at that time!"

Brenda gave the address, said her name was then Brenda Jones and then said bitterly, "And to think I sought you out specially to help me!"

"You dragged us into something that hasn't been pleasant, Mrs. Davison."

"I won't go back to that house! I'll go home instead."

"You'll string along with us or I dump you with the homicide squad. Take your choice." Brenda chose us.

In the ladies' room Brenda took off her scarf. Her hair in its pale braids looked perfectly neat. She seemed unaware of the stain on her sleeve. It was on the outside of the cuff which she wouldn't notice easily. I didn't call her attention to it. I took off my hat. My black curls were tousled and needed a proper doing which I now had no time for. Brenda admired my hat. She tried it on and looked like a dream. She was as delighted as an innocent kid. A strange woman! I felt jealous as I put the hat on again and she sighed enviously as she had to resume her white scarf.

Back in the restaurant Patrick was leaving the telephone booth.

"I had to report to the police that I'd found you," he said to Brenda.

"That isn't fair."

"I'm using a temporary police card. I have to report to the man in charge of your case. He won't let it go any further till I say so."

Brenda said, as we got into Tony Konrad's cab, and after Patrick had told him to take us out on Long Island, "Since you've told on me, I might as well go home at once."

"We'll drop you on the way," Patrick said. "But we're going on to that house at Sands Point just the same. A couple of policemen are in your apartment, so you'll have company."

Brenda shuddered. "All right. I'll stay with you."

"You're a coward."

She answered with some spirit. "Yes, I am. I'm afraid."

The glass panel was open. You could see Tony Konrad listening hard as he drove the cab swiftly along the lighted streets. I said, for his benefit, that I was glad Patrick was carrying a gun, for once. I told Brenda that Patrick was quicker on the draw than any cow man, using the double-quick method now in use by the F.B.I. Patrick sitting between me and Brenda, nudged me to shut up. Saying the wind was cold, he leaned forward and closed the panel.

"Some people talk too much," said he.

Tony took us across town on 23rd Street and turned north on lower Park Avenue. Ahead and ornamental like a lighted wedding cake the Grand Central Building straddled the wide street. We did not talk now. I sat watching the wedding cake speed toward us, and felt the thrill I always felt when driving like Superman directly through its middle. A red light stopped us briefly as we arrived at the northern exodus and the fashionable section of Park Avenue lay just ahead.

Patrick looked at his watch and opened the panel.

"Drive fast as the law allows soon as we cross the bridge, Tony. Stop for explicit directions when we get to Port Washington."

"Okay, Bud," Tony said happily.

Patrick closed the panel.

"Sure you don't want to go home?"

"Not under the circumstances," Brenda snapped.

The wind had risen and was fierce on the Queensborough Bridge. It made the elaborate ironwork sing like a procession of harps. Far below little whitecaps danced among the swaying red and green lights of the tugs and barges. The lighted city we were leaving was a fantasy in golden windows on deep indigo blue. Through a ventilating window in the cab came the spanking salt smell of seawater.

Down we sped among shadowy warehouses and on up a ramp to an elevated highway. Sometimes lights flew past, sometimes gray spaces. The sea came close, and lights from the shore jittered in black water. Residential sections with neat hedges and shrubbery-hidden houses slipped by. No one said anything. What a strange ride! Why were we making it? What had Brenda said or done that had induced Patrick to make this windy journey? Was it really to make certain that for once Brenda was telling the truth? Was she telling the truth? Had she stayed out there all day, just because she was afraid to jump out the window? Why jump? If she had blankets and a handy radiator or a bedpost she could let herself down. She had nerve enough, apparently. Her neatness—would anybody, if really subjected to the aloneness and the fear of a cold abandoned house, after such an abduction, put on her lipstick so precisely, braid so tidily her pale lovely hair? The truth itself is not believed from those who often have deceived. Well, I didn't always tell the truth, the whole truth, myself. Nobody did. Only if there was murder— murder! Dr. Crossland. Paula Eastwood. Who? *Who?* Why? The money. Naturally, somehow or other, the money. More often than for any other reason murder was done because of money. Money, money.

A flow of light behind us, timed to our speed, became obvious shortly after we drove through the edge of Great Neck. We lost it now and then. It closed in on us when we crossed the bridge over the inlet beyond Manhasset. Now it stuck along doggedly a few car lengths behind. As we rounded the curve into the fringes of Port Washington the car was close upon us. There was no doubt now that we were being tailed. Patrick ignored it. Brenda seemed not to notice.

Tony pulled up at a point where the water came close to the highway, and opened the panel. "Port Washington, Pat," he said. As he spoke a big black sedan roared around us and turned right up the hill a couple of blocks along.

A big black sedan! Von Osterholz, in Central Park, had used a big black sedan.

"Tell him where to go," Patrick ordered Brenda.

"Oh, please . . ."

"Tell him, and no monkey business, mind!"

Brenda gave instructions. The panel closed. We sped on, around an inlet, along a curving road. The black sedan was no longer following us.

We pulled up at a dark-red brick gatehouse with tall chimneys in the English manner. There was a wide iron-grilled gate for carriage use and a little one beside it for pedestrians. A lantern glowed dimly over the door of the house.

"Put on Jean's hat," Patrick said to Brenda, "and sit tight."

"But . . ."

"The gatekeeper may look us over. It's better if he doesn't recognize you. He'll phone the local police and we've trouble enough as it is. Put on the hat! Pull it forward, over your eyes."

I handed over my hat. Brenda put it on and tilted it forward. In the dim twilight in the cab which was the reflection of the headlights her mouth was sullen. Patrick, taking out his wallet with the police credentials as he moved, swung out of the cab and rang the bell of the gate house.

He came back quickly. An old man came out and opened the gate without even a glance in the cab.

We drove on. Brenda did not return the hat.

I felt sorry for her. Patrick's attitude toward her was merciless. He ordered her now to direct Tony to a spot near the house but off the drive where the cab wouldn't be easily seen either from the driveway or the Sound.

The house itself loomed suddenly. It was a Cape Cod house covered with weathered unpainted cedar shingles. Its closed windows were backed by closed Venetian blinds. Brenda directed Tony to a spot beside a willow tree away from the house. He turned the car facing the way he had come in and put out the lights. Patrick got out and, telling us to follow, started toward the house.

He didn't use the new torch. He didn't need it, because he can see in the dark like a cat. There was starlight. He went gliding along and Brenda followed and I followed Brenda, who still wore my hat. The sound of the high wind and heaving water filled the night with tremendous excitement.

The wind blew wildly, flinging the waves against the landing and the rocks. A vine rattled agonizingly against the shingled house. Across the black water, many miles away, the lights of small cities gleamed communally, but here in the rocking wind there was desolation and loneness. I felt afraid. My heart was pounding idiotically.

Patrick halted near the main entrance to the house and looked the situation over. The Sound lay on our left. Well away from the shore the running lights of a small boat rose and fell with the breakers. I shuddered, thinking of being in a small boat on a high sea.

"No blankets," Patrick said to Brenda. "No open window, either. Who closed it, if you jumped out as you said?"

She made no answer.

"You walked out a door of this house, if you were really ever in it. Another useless lie. Hand over your keys."

"They took my key. . . ."

Without another word Patrick grabbed Brenda's evening bag and fetched out the keys. He frisked her pockets also. He took something which he dropped in one pocket. A glove!

In the starlight which sufficed him he tried one after another key in the lock. None fitted. I suggested trying the back door and the French doors on the terrace. He answered tersely that they hadn't recently been opened. How could he tell in the dark, I wondered, as he took out his penknife and borrowed one of Brenda's strong hairpins and started picking the lock.

The boat bouncing on the breakers was closer in and heading this way. I shivered, watching it. Patrick picked away at the lock. Brenda stood in frozen silence. The wind swooped and howled and flung the water against the rocks. The vine scratched at the shingles which supported it.

The lock yielded.

Patrick took out the torch now and opened the door. He flashed the light into the entry, opened the second door into the hallway of the silent house, and flashed the light ahead of him.

He stopped abruptly.

On the floor at the foot of the stairway with its white balusters and mahogany railing lay sprawled the dead body of Felix von Osterholz.

Near its hand lay a revolver. As Patrick stooped over the corpse Brenda Davison ran forward and picked up the gun and wheeled upon us.

"Put up your hands!" she said.

"You *are* a fool!" Patrick said.

"Get upstairs!" Brenda said.

"Put down that gun!"

She made no move.

"I've got the torch and my gun is leveled on you. Put it down, I said."

Timidly she laid it on the carpet.

"Now *you* get upstairs!" Patrick said.

21

Patrick cocked his head and stood listening. He took out the gun, and slipped off the safety catch. He snapped off the torch. Soundlessly he moved back into the entry and stood just inside the front door, listening.

In the gruesome darkness I dared not move lest I stumble over the dead man.

Brenda had halted halfway upstairs.

She was standing there, hoping. She was intensely quiet, utterly motionless, she said not a word and emitted not even a sigh, but in that community of feeling which comes in the stress of great danger I knew she was pleased about something.

Someone who wished us evil was coming here and Brenda was expecting it with pleasure. Nothing but her immediate fear of Patrick and his gun stopped her from running out of this house and screaming with triumph.

A boat bumped against the landing. A chain clanked. Above the roar of wind and water a thick voice sounded.

"Jesus Christ! What a sea! Lucky to get here at all, we are!"

There was no reply.

Patrick listened from the partly open door. The wind blew and the water roared and the vine went on scraping the house, but all at once this place seemed silent as a tomb. The tomb of Felix von Osterholz, at the moment.

Brenda now also stood and listened. She was content.

I was aware for the first time of her perfume, that light gay scent, which had chosen this moment to assert itself. And I wasn't jealous any longer. I hated her!

Footsteps were audible on the landing, which jutted into the water from a terrace extending slightly to the right of the front entrance of the house.

Patrick closed the door, slipped through the entry, closed the second door, and, holding the revolver in his right hand, clasped my arm with the left. He guided me around the body and up the stairs.

He can see in the dark like a cat. And he was watching Brenda.

"Get on upstairs, Mrs. Davison!" She did not move. "All the way up!" he said.

"Well, why not?" she said. She lilted it. She was happy. She ran softly up the flight to the landing.

We moved up behind her as far as the landing, which was more than half-way to the second floor.

"All the way up," Patrick ordered Brenda. "Stay in the hall. We'll wait on the landing. And keep quiet."

Brenda, wearing my fine flowery hat, obeyed without answering. She obeyed like one utterly carefree. The upstairs hall was about eight or nine steps beyond the landing. Brenda stopped beside the railing around the stair well. There she could watch the front door.

Patrick ordered me to the rear of the landing and crouched on his heels in front of me at a point where he could watch both Brenda and the lower hall. He had the unlit torch in his left hand. In the right he held the revolver.

There was a short wait, though a longer one than he anticipated. I wondered if the men were searching the premises. Would they find Tony Konrad? Or was he waiting for them? Tipping them off? How crazy Pat had been to let him come here! Crazy!

A key was put in the lock of the front door. A band of light gleamed under the inner door from the entry. The door opened while the outside door was still open and a chilly blast of air swept through the hall. The outside door closed.

"Hell of a night for a job like this," the thick voice said. "I don't want to go back in that sea. Why not leave them lay?"

The first man—was it a man?—said nothing. Slowly he, or she, allowed the torchlight to creep over the body at the foot of the stairs.

The thick voice asked, "He's okay where he is, ain't he?" His voice sounded dry. He was worried. "Two of 'em," he mumbled. "What's the matter with leaving 'em where they are?" He was pleading. But the other said nothing. He was now holding the torch focused on the dead man's face. It looked clean as wax. The black brows flared across the waxen forehead and the auburn hair was neat. The eyes were closed and so was the mouth. A brown splotch slightly marred the left side of the forehead.

The thick-voiced man stepped forward. He was now clearly visible in the edge of the light from the torch. He was short, but powerfully built. A wet brown felt hat was pulled low over what seemed a thick-featured face. He wore a yellow slicker which glistened from sea water. "Hey?" he asked. "What goes on here? First time I ever see a suicide with eyes and mouth shut. He wasn't lefthanded, either." The thick voice thickened. "What about that dame?"

The other still did not answer. He began slowly wheeling the light around the hall.

It focused on each part of the hall in turn. I saw the gray-and-white striped paper, the mahogany console, the classic sunburst mirror, two Duncan Phyfe chairs, white-enameled woodwork, a green carpet. I saw the revolver when the torch found it and fastened on it.

The gun which Brenda had picked up and put down was a good forty inches from where it had been when we came in. This evidently bothered the one holding the torch.

The other stooped beside the body and took hold of an arm. "Stiff as a rod," he growled. "Once we got it out there it would sink like a rock. Us too, maybe."

The one with the torch inched forward, took out an ugly short-barreled automatic pistol and leveled it on the stooping man's powerful back. The hand holding the gun was gloved.

Now the silence was ghastly. The thick-voiced man squatting beside the rigid body of von Osterholz made an easy target. But the other took extra cautious aim. He didn't dare to bungle. The first shot must tell.

The light seemed to stay focused interminably on the man's wide powerful back. The face and figure of the one holding the torch, the one getting ready to kill, stayed darkly shadowed.

In the silence I could hear Patrick's watch tick.

Then Brenda Davison screamed.

The gun slid back into shadow. The stooping man sprang up. The torchlight sped, incredibly swift, up the stairs, passed the landing, fastened, on my hat, bending on Brenda's head above the second-floor railing. The ugly automatic barked and the bullet which might have killed the stooping man got Brenda. The hat came tumbling down. The man whom death had just passed by snatched out another gun and started shooting wildly. Gunshots zinged and thudded. Patrick crept forward and fired between the balusters. The thick-voice man yelled. He jumped backwards and jostled the torch. It fell and lay rocking sideways on the carpet. Its switch was locked, it remained alight, but it kept moving and the area it lighted swayed crazily.

Again ordering me to the back of the landing Patrick fired a second shot. A gun fell to the floor, and Patrick went over the railing, dropped, landed, kicked the gun away as the thick-voiced man grabbed for it. The man straightened up and hit Patrick. Patrick hit him back. The man hit him in the stomach. Patrick staggered, crouched, and sprang and hit the man in the jaw. The man tottered, whirled about, and hit Patrick over the heart. Patrick recoiled, and got the man in the right shoulder as he came on, and then they grappled and rolled in a clinch, all the time slugging each other.

I had not moved back on the landing. I hung on hard to the smooth mahogany railing and I watched the fight. They were fighting in half-shadow. The torch had ceased to sway but all its light was concentrated on that part of the carpet close to the base-board of the staircase directly below where I watched. The two men slugged and grunted and all the time kept squirming toward the wedge of brightness.

I had forgotten the other till I saw him moving up with the gun. He halted, and took deliberate aim. At Patrick? I could not tell. It occurred to me indeed that he didn't care which man he picked off first, but, as before, he took time, daring not to miss. He? Definitely.

I started down the stairs. My foot squashed something. The hat. I was close enough to see the man's finger flatten on the trigger. Again he waited. He shifted the gun slightly. He fired. I heard the gunshot. I turned then and saw the man with the thick voice and heavy shoulders roll gently into the wedge of light. He lay still. The man with the gun took aim again. Patrick was rising, crouching. He dived forward and kicked the torch so that its light swung about to focus on the man with the gun. He was Harold Couch. My foot touched the squashy thing again and I grabbed it up and flung it and a moment later the gun seemed to explode inside it.

"Thus ended a good hat," I said.

"That one's very nice," Ellen said.

"Macy's. Nine ninety-four," I said.

"Good thing Jean packed a mean hat," Patrick said. "I'd dropped both my gun and my flashlight in the scuffle. If the hat hadn't spoiled his aim Couch would have popped me off too. The old boy's right handy with a gun."

"What a fiend!" Ellen said, with a shudder. "Such a nice quiet-seeming man, too."

"That's what I thought, Ellen. Pat knew he was the one all along. But not me. My goodness!"

We were having a drink in the King Cole Room at the St. Regis. Hank was to join us here, and we would go on to Luchow's for dinner. Five days had passed since Ellen had said that any time would do for this cocktail.

"What happened then?" Ellen asked.

Patrick said, "Then Tony turned up. Not bloody, but unbowed."

"The idiot had taken a nap in his cab," I said.

Patrick said, "Couch didn't spot the cab when he and his boy friend scouted round the house before coming in to finish the dirty work. Tony had got it well hidden behind some shrubbery."

"Tony almost missed the showdown," I said. "But was I glad to see him! Pat had grabbed Couch by then and had got the gun. But Tony came in handy. He went to fetch the police. He'll get the reward."

"He rates it," Patrick said. "He found the glove on the landing. He tailed von Osterholz after he suspected him of tailing us. He heard him tell a cab driver to drop him at 89th and York. Stuff like that."

"Tony just goes to show that there are people in New York who do things out of simple curiosity, same as any place else," I said. "He was just sticking round for the fun."

"He's okay," Patrick said.

"Patrick has a lot of confidence in people," I said. "Well, in a way, so do I, but somehow I trust the wrong people. I trusted that snake of a Harold Couch."

Ellen said, "Tony wouldn't've gotten very far if Pat hadn't been there to make something of the clues."

"I take a bow," Patrick said. "All the same, we couldn't've done without him. There he was, all the time. He did a lot of first-rate leg work, Ellen."

Ellen asked, "Who was following you in the black sedan? When you went out to Sands Point?"

"The police," Patrick said. "They were tailing Tony. When we stopped on the edge of Port Washington they passed us and turned up the hill, so that Tony wouldn't catch on. But they lost our trail. They picked it up again and had got to the gate-house just before Tony got back there on his way to phone them to come and get Couch."

"How about Brenda?" Ellen asked.

"She'll be okay," Patrick said. "Mild concussion. Shock. Couch's bullet grazed her right temple. Probably would have killed her, but for that hat."

"Um-m," Ellen said.

I said, "Does she make you feel jealous, Ellen?"

"Intensely," Ellen said. "At my age I ought to have more sense."

"At any age one should," I said. "When I think how dumb she was, being so silly about what she called social advantages and stuff like that. By the way, when Couch banged away at her he thought she was me. Because of the hat. She was leaning over the railing upstairs, you see, and she had on my hat."

"Lovely hat," Ellen said.

"Um-m," I said. "But expensive."

"No hat that saves lives should be called expensive," Patrick said. "Have you heard that Pete and Anne are taking Katy and Brenda with them out West? Just the thing for Brenda. She never will snap out of it entirely so long as she's around Liz Ashbrook."

"I expect not," Ellen said.

"Liz Ashbrook amuses me, though," I said. "It's not her heart. It's her liver. She says Clive would be bored if she babbled about her liver. So she calls it a heart. That was a fainting spell she had in her hotel. Not a heart attack."

"Women are funny," Patrick said. "Can't see what they see in Ashbrook myself."

"He's very good-looking," Ellen said.

I said, "Yes. Well, really Brenda is to blame for the whole mess. If she hadn't tried to be so mysterious about her past! Just because she didn't want

Liz to know that her name had been Brenda Jones and she'd grown up in a whistle-stop and disliked the aunt that raised her."

Patrick said, "You might even say that Liz herself is to blame, darling. Brenda wouldn't have fallen for the Felix von Osterholz business to start with if Liz Ashbrook hadn't dazzled her so. She thought the guy must be hot stuff or he wouldn't have intrigued the fascinating Liz. Yet Liz would give anything to look like Brenda."

"A face isn't much good without a brain," said Ellen.

"Handier than a brain without face, darling," I said.

"Anyway, the face spoiled Couch's well-laid plans," Patrick said. "The phony Osterholz went nuts over the face. Pulled a doublecross and murdered his own wife—Paula Eastwood—and fixed her up to look like Brenda, meaning to decamp with Brenda and her jewels, as well as the twenty grand Couch was to pay him for doing her in. He must have planned the details of Paula's murder very carefully in advance. There was only about forty minutes between the time he was in our hotel room and Couch's phoning that Brenda was missing from home. In forty minutes Osterholz went from the Waldorf to Paula Eastwood's, murdered her, smashed up her face, painted her fingernails, went back to Brenda's and took her away. Fast work, even at an hour with little traffic."

"The thing you'd think would take the most time was putting on the nail polish," I said. "But, after all, he was a beauty operator himself. Paula's shop back in Vienna was a branch of his own in Berlin."

Ellen said, "I understand the police laboratory found Paula's usual shade of polish under Brenda's cinnamon-red."

"He thought of everything. Even to the glove," I said. "And leaving Paula's front door unlocked, hoping her body would be found promptly so that he would appear to have kept his bargain, even though not in the way Couch expected. Osterholz had been told to knock Brenda in the head and dump her body in the Sound. By the way, Ellen, the glove found in Paula's apartment was not the mate to the one Brenda dropped on the landing. Pat found the mate to the one on the landing in her pocket there at her house when he frisked her for keys. She had several pairs specially made for her, all just alike. Osterholz had got one somehow, in advance, purposely to leave in Paula's apartment for Couch and the police. He happened to leave a left glove and Brenda happened to drop a right glove on the landing."

"How awful!" Ellen cried. "And how dumb! Where could he have taken her even if he had got away with it? No place!"

"Typical German mind," Patrick said. "Undervalues everything not German. Hadn't the foggiest notion that New York police were any good. Had managed to sneak into the country illegally and imagined he could sneak out the same way with Brenda. Thought he could snatch Brenda, and she'd actually like it. Strong-arm German stuff."

"If Paula was so clever," Ellen asked, "why did she have anything to do with this so-called Osterholz?"

"He was her husband back in Germany. His real name was Wagner. Paula was planted in this country, before the war, as an enemy agent. She came in on a forged passport under the name of Osterholz. And Osterholz—as we'll call Wagner, since we're used to the name Osterholz—was also here without proper authority. They were stuck with each other. Either could turn the other in. He didn't live at her place, didn't dare risk it. But she had to receive him. Even if she may not have wanted to, she gave him a key. And both were at the mercy of the man who wanted to get rid of Brenda."

"Brenda is dumb," I said.

"Brenda was scared," Pat said, as if correcting me.

"She's said to be smart about money," Ellen said.

"People smart about money are often dumb about people," I said. "Couch was the only one in that crowd she really trusted. Not that I should talk."

"If people only wouldn't lie so," Ellen said then.

"In all murder cases there is lying and concealment of evidence and stuff like that," said Patrick. "Everybody lied in this case. Even Anne lied a little, out of loyalty to Brenda. Pete lied, out of loyalty to Anne. He did ride the trains and behave in a pretty dizzy sort of way, but he lied when he said Anne broke their date."

"They're in love," I said. As usual.

Hank Rawlings showed up and we had more drinks. Patrick outlined the story for Hank, telling him about the pseudo-Osterholz and his wife Paula who had to agree or else to the scheme to abduct and murder Brenda and therefore got murdered herself. He told Hank about the gatecrashers and stolen love letters. Both were deliberately planned to hurt Brenda's reputation so that when she turned up murdered people would say it was the company she kept. Osterholz wrote the letters and by that time he was putting his heart in the work because he had fallen for Brenda. Couch got the idea of having Wagner pretend to be Felix von Osterholz because he knew that Brenda had heard about the affair and was impressed with everything connected with Liz. He looked enough like the real Osterholz to explain any questions by blaming the war. The only disguise he used was to dye his hair auburn and his heavy eyebrows black. Also, Liz was pretty sure to avoid anybody named Osterholz if she got onto Brenda's seeing him because Clive was jealous.

"That's the way it worked, too," I said. "After the party Elizabeth phoned Pat to ask him to find von Osterholz. Later she called again, but Pat hadn't time to talk just then. By the next day she didn't want to find the man, said she was afraid she'd get the immigration officers after him or something. As a matter of fact all that worried her was Clive's jealousy."

The showdown, that is, the date for murdering Brenda, was stepped up because Pete Davison came East and was trying to talk Brenda into going to Arizona.

"She was too smart about money, that was it," Patrick said.

"And, of course," I said, "after the agranulocystosis thing she got suspicious. Couch thought she sensed what he was up to."

"Cy," Patrick said. "Agranulocytosis."

"Good God!" Hank cried. "What's that?"

"Too many of the wrong corpuscles," I said.

"Too few of the right ones," Patrick said.

"But how? Why? When? Who?"

Patrick said, "An attempt was made on Brenda's life a few months ago. Pyramidon, which is deadly in her case, was planted among aspirin tablets. Her doctor, Crossland, discovered it, accused the would-be murderer, and got himself murdered. In his office. With his own gun. It was called suicide."

"How did you get onto that?" Hank asked.

I said, "Doctors aren't so ethical they won't mention an exciting diagnosis to an old friend. So when Couch told us that Crossland had been his own doctor for thirty years Pat suspected that the doctor had told Couch about Brenda's peculiar susceptibility to pyramidon, and that when Katy almost died of the same sort of thing that he had accused Couch and so got himself murdered."

Patrick said, "Couch was afraid to try the same method on Brenda again. So he hired Osterholz, who doublecrossed him, killed his wife, fixed her up to be identified as Brenda, and kidnapped Brenda. That guy Couch had no real luck."

"How did he get on to Osterholz?" Hank asked.

"Paula went to Couch to see about getting a job for her husband. She knew all about the Davison family, of course. Her contact with Liz went back a good many years. Couch sensed what was up, accused them both of having been spies, and ordered Osterholz to do what he wanted, or else."

"Why would Osterholz go to that party?" Hank asked then.

"Brenda had never permitted him to come to her apartment. The murder was set for that night. Couch ordered Osterholz to come to the party to get the layout of the place. In the crowd Brenda might not even see him. But Osterholz got cold feet, drugged himself as he'd done in the war when facing danger, took too much, and brought on the heart attack."

"Which our Patrick spotted," I said. "Thereby making Pat himself somebody to be got rid of. Along with being suspected of being hired by Brenda, too. So Couch told Osterholz to get Pat out of the way, too. He muffed it. Twice."

"He was cool enough when he felt safe," Pat said. "He did a smooth job with that cinnamon nail polish."

"How did he get into the penthouse when he went for Brenda?" Ellen asked.

"Through the kitchen door. No chain was put on it at night because the servants let themselves in early mornings. He took Brenda out the front door, but changed his mind and marched her back and used the service lift to go down, which was how he'd come up. At first we felt suspicious of the sulky new elevator man, but no dice."

"Couch always seemed a swell guy," Hank said.

"Too fond of money," Patrick said.

"But he had plenty, and was getting on, and had no one any more to spend it on," Ellen said.

"There are people like that about money," Patrick said. "It's greed."

I said, "He took advantage of the family bickering. Used a forged power of attorney. Appropriated funds scheduled for reinvestment. Stuck them for more taxes than he passed along."

"Don't blame them," Patrick said. "Their father had taught them they hadn't sense enough to handle money. Old Davison assumed that Harold Couch was honest because his father was. But when old Mr. Davison died and old Mr. Couch retired our friend Hal had a free hand. He interpreted the will to suit himself knowing that neither Pete nor Liz would question anything. But Brenda was different. She sensed that her own position was shaky if Liz and Pete ganged up against her and she kept asking questions. Couch got panicked."

"What about that story Mr. Couch told us about her childhood?" I asked.

"That was the best his detectives dug up. It was Couch who put the dicks on her tail, not old Mr. Davison."

"Is there any money left?" Ellen asked.

"Plenty."

"Couch won't need money where he's going," Hank said.

"He won't burn, after that full confession," Patrick said.

"He still won't need much money," Hank said.

"Money is the root of all evil," I said. "I like it, though."

"When did he find out that Osterholz had doublecrossed him?" Hank asked.

"He started being suspicious when the body was found in Paula Eastwood's apartment instead of somewhere in Long Island Sound."

"He didn't suspect that the body wasn't Brenda's. He identified it, didn't he?"

"Yes. You see, the hair was the same. And the rinse Paula used for Brenda's hair was the one she used herself. The women were close to the same size, too. So Couch was suspicious only because Osterholz hadn't done the job in the way planned."

I said, "Mr. Couch is *not* an artist. Like Pat. He didn't spy straight off that Paula's curves couldn't possibly be Brenda's."

Patrick let that pass. "But he did sense that his gunman had fallen for the gal, so he was worried. Then the other man, whose name was Berger, called on Couch. Berger was in a spot himself now. He'd been trusted with the jewels. They were phony. He was afraid to go back to Osterholz at the Sands Point house and say so because he thought he'd be called a liar and liquidated. Incidentally, he had to see Couch anyhow to collect for the job. He was to take Couch's dough to Osterholz along with what he got from the fence for the ice. Couch told Berger to wait till dark and to keep the boat handy and he'd get in touch then. In the meantime he went out to Sands Point and shot Osterholz."

"Just think," I said. "When we were lunching with Mr. Couch at Longchamps, and eating duckling and such, all the time he sat there plotting to leave for Sands Point the minute he got rid of us. He drove out, drove to the beach along the lane not much used at this time of year, made his way along the shore to Brenda's house, was admitted by Osterholz, wormed out the truth, and shot the guy. Brenda woke up. She was really shut in, up in that room, and she'd fallen asleep. Osterholz had been afraid to let her out till Berger got back with the dough, after which he was going to take her away by force, if she wouldn't go willingly."

"Brenda pounded on the door," Pat said. "Couch went up and opened it and told her he had had to shoot Osterholz in self-defense. He talked her into staying in the house till dark. He said he would come back and move the body elsewhere so that there would be no scandal. A scandal would mean losing Katy—the old technique, see!"

"She fell for it," I said. "She let him lock her in so that if anybody discovered her there she could say she was abducted and locked in. She was to swear that the other thug had killed Osterholz. But as evening started closing in she got scared. She never once suspected Couch's framing her. She was simply scared of staying in that place in the dark with a dead man downstairs, so used some tweezers from her make-up kit and managed to turn the key locking her in, and got out. By the time she got to town she had cold feet about seeing Mr. Couch, so she came to Pat."

"By way of Tony Konrad," Pat said.

"Why didn't Couch shoot her after shooting Osterholz?" Hank asked.

"He was afraid he might have been seen going to the house. He'd rather take a chance on keeping her there till night, when he could polish her off, along with the strong-armed Berger after he'd dumped Osterholz and Brenda in the Sound. 'Two of them,' Berger kept saying, when they came into the house that night. Couch had told Berger that Osterholz had killed Brenda and shot himself. It didn't matter what Berger found out after they got there. He wasn't too bright and he was scheduled to be shot anyway. But the wind had come up and Couch himself was afraid to go back in the boat so he decided to do away with Berger right in the house and then shoot Brenda and leave the bodies there and slip away along the shore and after that let come what may. Only Brenda screamed just as he was about to shoot Berger in the back. That did it."

"There was a wonderful fight," I said. "Pat won it."

"The fight was won by a hat," Patrick said.

I said, "Pat, you told me you didn't know that was a bloodstain on Brenda's sleeve. There at the restaurant. You said it could have been ketchup."

"Sure," Patrick said. "Also, it could be a bloodstain. She touched Osterholz's face when she came down. The blood was then still gooey."

"You were smart to go out there, Pat," Ellen said.

"Routine. And when she bucked it, a must."

"Why routine? You mean a hunch, don't you?" Hank asked.

"Nope. Couch mentioned the house the first time Brenda's absence came up. Why? Because it was on his mind. He said she *wouldn't* go there, with no lights or water and so on. I had my eye on him, anyhow. As my friend Detective Lieutenant Dorn of the New York Police said, nobody knows as much about people as the man who handles their money. Couch knew more than most. These clients wouldn't even come to New York to see him. He went to them. I figured he had known von Osterholz, the real one, and maybe Paula Eastwood, too, back in Europe. It was Couch who told us that Brenda had not renewed the insurance on her jewelry. How come? Why hadn't he insisted? Well, with what he had on his mind, maybe he wanted to reduce any hazards. Insurance companies have smart dicks. But the thing that tied it was Crossland's death previously and the agranulocytosis."

"There you go again," Hank said.

"Cy," I said, to remember it. "The poor old doctor."

"And poor little Katy. Almost," Ellen said.

"Poor everybody. Even Clive Ashbrook," I said.

"I know," Ellen said. "I feel sorry for him somehow."

"Me, too."

"Oh, my God!" cried Pat and Hank. Then Hank said, "Smart work, Pat. Calls for another round." He signaled the order to the waiter. "Couch must be crazy. Imagine plotting to deprive this ugly world of a face like Brenda Davison's."

"Terrible," Patrick said.

Ellen and I exchanged looks.

THE END

About the Rue Morgue Press

"Rue Morgue Press is the old-mystery lover's best friend, reprinting high quality books from the 1930s and '40s."
—*Ellery Queen's Mystery Magazine*

Since 1997, the Rue Morgue Press has reprinted scores of traditional mysteries, the kind of books that were the hallmark of the Golden Age of detective fiction. Authors reprinted or to be reprinted by the Rue Morgue include Catherine Aird, Delano Ames, H. C. Bailey, Morris Bishop, Nicholas Blake, Dorothy Bowers, Pamela Branch, Joanna Cannan, John Dickson Carr, Glyn Carr, Torrey Chanslor, Clyde B. Clason, Joan Coggin, Manning Coles, Lucy Cores, Frances Crane, Norbert Davis, Elizabeth Dean, Carter Dickson, Eilis Dillon, Michael Gilbert, Constance & Gwenyth Little, Marlys Millhiser, Gladys Mitchell, Patricia Moyes, James Norman, Stuart Palmer, Craig Rice, Kelley Roos, Charlotte Murray Russell, Maureen Sarsfield, Margaret Scherf, Juanita Sheridan and Colin Watson..

To suggest titles or to receive a catalog of Rue Morgue Press books write 87 Lone Tree Lane, Lyons, CO 80540, telephone 800-699-6214, or check out our website, www.ruemorguepress.com, which lists complete descriptions of all of our titles, along with lengthy biographies of our writers.